Phantom of my Heart
A two-part phan-fic based on the 2004 film version of Phantom of the Opera
By Sarah B. Wilkins

Dedication

Firstly, I dedicate this to the housekeeping crew at Cold Spring Resort in Ashland, NH, which I was a part of for 10 years. It was there in the stories told that I first became inspired to write this. Though I no longer am there, I will forever consider you all part of my family.

I also dedicate this to Gerard Butler. As with all my phanfics, I attribute the depth of my inspiration to his portrayal of Erik/The Phantom. He climbed so far deeply into this role that all I have to do is look at his eyes at any given moment and understand what is going through the character's mind and heart right then and there. Thank you, Gerry, for giving of your talent in this movie.

Author's Note

Dear readers,

What you are about to read is a work that has taken me multiple years to write. As such, despite proofreading and editing efforts, you may find that the flow or style may change as the story unfolds. I have written a few other stories while this project was in progress, and so naturally my own style/maturity as a writer continued to develop and change in the process.

Because this story line has taken so long to write, and because it is probably my most personal phanfic, I have decided to publish both as a stand-alone part of my A Phantom Heart Series collection. It will take me some time and effort to switch gears from this plot and begin work on future stories or published collections.

I do hope you enjoy reading this 'phantasy' of mine. I believe I am not the only Phantom phan who has thought down this path of "what if...?"

~Sarah B. Wilkins

Phantom of the Resort

****PROLOGUE****

    I first heard the stories about the haunted rental unit two months after being hired into the housekeeping team at Misty Brook Resort. "Someone died there," they said. "Sometimes he'll visit the rec room in the basement of the office building." At first, I kind of shrugged it off. After all, my group didn't normally clean that section of two-story condos.
    But over the course of the next year or so, things began to happen that got me thinking that perhaps there was in fact something to these rumors. Random objects were flung across the room when only one girl was upstairs and the sliding doors to the balcony were closed and locked. Lights in the rec room would flicker, and yet the security cameras never picked anyone up. A couple times, the vacuum would turn itself on when no one was around it. Once, when I was waiting alone in the housekeeping shed for my ride at the end of the day, the lights turned off by themselves without being on a timer.
    Then, it grew all the more suspicious. Units that were supposed to be clean would be checked only to find the beds or sofas at least sat upon, dishes missing one week and then too many of something else the next. Towels and extra sheets that we housekeepers knew for a fact had been left in the units we cleaned were reported missing. What really added to the confusion was the fact that not all of the tricks were negative, at least, not entirely. Things would be reported as needing repair, but when the maintenance men went to check them out, they'd be fixed. If it weren't for the other mysterious occurrences, we housekeepers would surely be accused of simply trying to get a unit closed "for repair" just to get out of cleaning it. Night security had no

explanation, and cameras in the units were out of the question.

So there was a meeting. Who was going to spend a week in that unit? No one volunteered, claiming they had too many other things going on. That's when I spoke up out of complete curiosity and my sense of adventure. Within what seemed like half of a second, I had the keys in my hand along with a bunch of gift cards and vouchers (which I suspect they would have used to bribe someone if I hadn't spoken up) before I was practically shoved out the door to go home and pack. *Sheesh!* I thought to myself.

Within a few hours, I was all settled in. Everything seemed normal, and so I decided to explore further than I could ever have searched when cleaning. It wasn't until I was peering into the upstairs walk-in closet that I noticed anything unusual. There was a little trap door in the ceiling, unhooked. I would have dismissed it as a simple oversight by the maintenance men, but then I heard the faintest, yet unmistakable sound of squeaking metal; it seemed to grow louder the longer I listened. *Gotcha...* I smirked, grabbing a chair to give me a boost up. In theory, it would have worked. I managed to get the door open and my arms through, but in my attempt to lift myself up, I kicked the chair away. "Oh great. Help..? I know you're up here...C'mon, help..!" I struggled to keep my grip.

"Why should I lend you aid in ruining my fun?" A smirking voice finally replied moments before his masked face appeared. As he grabbed hold of my wrists, I gasped.

"Y–you're...the Phantom of the–"

"Resort." He cut me off stubbornly.

"But–"

"I'll let you go." He threatened.

"But...I *know* you..." That was the last I could manage before the **THUNK**. And the pain. And the darkness.

****

****ONE****

I awoke with a groan. Glancing around, I knew I was no longer in the unit. At least, not part of the unit I'd ever seen. It had to have been the attic, dimly lit by a single, battery-powered lantern sitting on a shelf. Shadows flickered in front of it as the alleged Resort Ghost moved around just out of my sight, the metallic squeaking continuing to pierce any further investigating thought. "Headache..." I winced and closed my eyes again, attempting to lift my arm so I could rub the pain away. My arm wouldn't budge though, and I reluctantly opened my eyes to see the precise reason why. *I don't believe it. Here I am, injured, and he's gone and tied me up!* As if on cue, he crouched down next to where I was lying on the floor. "You're awake..."

"Yes, no thanks to you..." I glared up at him. "I can't believe you actually did that!"

"Mademoiselle, if you really know me as you claim, then you'd know I'm a man of my word."

"True enough, but I also know you *are* a man, not a monster, and deep down inside, you know how cruel it is to bind up an injured innocent woman like this." He clearly wasn't expecting that tone out of me, because once the shock left his face, he undid the ropes. Except they weren't ropes. They were the strings we used to tie the bundles of clean linen together. "So that explains their constant disappearances..." I observed.

"Yes, and had I not scared you out of the shed that one day, you would have seen me take them." His tone was annoyingly casual, as if he kidnapped housekeepers regularly. "You will get the answers you undoubtedly seek in due time. But as you are my prisoner, I'll be the one who does all the asking." Crossing his legs, he dangled the strings in front of my nose, alerting me to the frustrating fact that it was beginning to itch. Before I could even wrinkle said nose, he continued. "Now, suppose you tell me just how you know me so well?" He began bouncing the strings up and down, causing them to lightly brush against(and do absolutely nothing to relieve the itch of) my nose.

"Erm...how familiar are you with the TVs here...?"

"Was that a question...?" *Bounce. Bounce. Bounce.*

"Do you want to be able to understand my answer or not?" *Oops.* Too late. The bouncing turned into tapping. "Fine. Try to keep up, Monsieur Literal." I glared, knowing full well he absolutely knew how itchy my nose was. He had to. "I saw your story in the form of a movie countless times, read about you, wrote about you, watched the movie some more..."

"...I see..." *That's it? No indication as to how much of that he understood??* As if reading my mind, he stood up and began to pace. Either I'd answered quicker than he expected, or he didn't want to admit his confusion. Whatever his reason, he was distracted enough for me to seize the opportunity. I flung my hand up to scratch my nose...and immediately regretted it. The resulting yelp of pain paired with a sneeze caused him to jump, hitting his head on the ceiling.

"**Mademoiselle do you mind being silent while I am thinking??**"

"...but that was a sneeze..." I sniffled, rubbing my nose and my injured arm at the same time. Unamused, he stormed over to me.

"**Do not. Try. My patience!**" Apparently my response was to look at him so pitifully that he immediately softened before returning to his crouched position. "Now then. Obviously, you know far too much, and so you will remain my prisoner for the time being. I know all about that meeting, and that you're here to report any and all sightings. I cannot let that happen. However, seeing as you're...not in the best shape for my usual treatment, I'll postpone it until you've sufficiently mended."

"So, in other words, you're eventually going to try *your* patient?" At this, he glared more intensely than I'd ever seen him glare before. "...sorry..." I bit my lip but giggled inside at my little joke. In the silence that followed, I glanced around to visually explore the attic space. But since I was lying flat on my back aside from one of the thinner spare pillows under my head, I couldn't see much. I did, however, spot the cause of the squeaking sound; I had apparently caught him in the middle of reshaping one of the stove burners which frequently got bent if something exceptionally heavy was put on top of them. When I looked his way again, his smirk had returned.

"Don't try to sit up until I've thoroughly examined you." From the look on his face, I knew he was going to be less than gentle.

My assumption proved correct. Countless yelps and a sore throat later, he determined I had in fact dislocated my arm(which he proceeded to fix immediately without so much as a warning about the pain), broken my other wrist, and bruised several bones in my back, hips, and legs. Not to mention the bump on my head from hitting it on the toppled-over chair. From the loss of my voice, I was surprised he hadn't used the first shredded rag as a 'bandage' over my mouth. Perhaps he figured that now, at last I'd be silent. The bandaging process was more gentle and focused, as if he were trying to remember instructions from a book he'd read long ago. I still couldn't believe he was really there...the Phantom of the Opera...I think he could see all the questions building up inside me....how he'd gotten there, how he hadn't aged a bit despite the fact that the rumors had been going around the resort for years...what his plans for me were...

But if he could read the questions in my mind, he wasn't about to answer them anytime soon. He was enjoying the silence. Perhaps he was right. I'd invaded his space. Ruined his fun. *Then why keep me here?*

I must have fallen asleep, because the next thing I knew, he was lifting my head just enough to pour ice cold water past my lips. Not realizing until then just how thirsty I was, I gulped the whole thing down before opening my eyes to meet his concerned gaze. *Concern? How long was I asleep?* "You never told me your name..." I blinked at his abruptness, but then figured it was his own way of testing my voice's recovery.

"Sarah..." I managed hoarsely.

"And I suppose I needn't tell you mine..."

"It...*is* Erik, right?"

"Well then...apparently you know more than I expected..." He scowled bitterly, leaning back in his chair. "I thought you were going to say O.G., after which I would have corrected you by saying R.G."

"Don't start that again..." I rolled my eyes. "I also know what happened and why you would want to leave..."

"That's about as far as you're going to go." He glared. "You need not wear your voice out again. As much as it pains me to admit, silence has become boring over the past two days."

"Two—? That's how long...?"

"You hit your head, remember..."

"Right..." As if on cue, the bump decided to throb with pain right then and there. At my wince, he rose to his feet.

"More water, I take it?"

"Please...?" As he left the room, I realized I'd been returned to the unit's familiarity. He'd placed me on a twin-size bed rather than the master queen, but as he said, I was still a prisoner. Upon his return, he set both a glass of water as well as a plated sandwich on top of the dresser beside me.

"Amazing to see what this one guest left behind in her sudden disappearance..." His smirk had come back, and it took me a moment to process the weight of what he'd just said.

"You really mean to keep me here..." I voiced my deduction.

"Well, not *here* exactly...Other guests will want to rent this unit..." As the smirk grew, I knew I had to think quickly.

"Yes, eventually...depending on how long the investigation takes..."

"Investigation...?"

"Mmhmm...You know, the one where all the police and maintenance men come in and out, tearing every crevice apart until I'm found..." I couldn't help but let my own smirk show. "If *I* found you, they certainly will..." At the sudden change of expression, he clearly(and surprisingly) hadn't thought of that. "On the other hand, I could help you on the outside...kind of like Madame Giry...I could put what you tell me to in my report to keep your fun going..."

"Perhaps...Except how would you explain your injuries?"

"Well, I *did* fall, did I not?" I didn't even blink.

"So you did..." he lost his smirk once more. "But you have yet to prove that I can trust you."

"And how do you propose I do that, when I can't even pick up that sandwich?" I flailed my bandaged arms as best as I could, resulting instead as a very poor impression of a penguin dreaming of flight. For a moment, his smirk reappeared. *He wouldn't...* My eyes widened at the thought of him taunting me by eating it in front of me. As if on cue, my stomach growled in panic, and Erik sighed. Sitting back down next to my bed, he fed me the sandwich. I dared not say anything about his kind gesture lest he shove the whole thing down my throat. *If he's to trust me, I cannot test him...*

****

When I next awoke, he was sitting on the opposite bed, reclined against the wall, and fiddling with my camera. Intrigued, I decided to keep silent so I could watch him figure it out on his own. He'd first managed to look back through the pictures I'd already taken, and was now pressing the right button to turn it on fully. I almost let out a giggle at his surprised expression at the lens popping out towards his face, but he recovered too quickly. A slight frown appeared as he examined the glass, then he slid his hand into his pocket to pull out a handkerchief. Another piece of cloth came with it, however, and dropped to the floor somewhat heavily. As he reached down to retrieve it, something clicked inside my mind. "...Hey, that's the missing sock a guest kept hounding us to find!" Startled at the sound of my voice, he fumbled with it as he struggled to keep his balance. At that moment, a small, quarter-sized object flung itself out of the sock and landed on the floor between the two beds. Upon closer inspection, I could make out glittery deep blue petals of sculpted metal with a pearl in the middle of it. "What a pretty rose..." I absentmindedly started to reach for it, forgetting that I was temporarily armless.

"**Don't touch it!**" He pounced on it with such suddenness that he's fortunate I didn't jump backwards through the wall.

Instead, I lost my balance, rolling off the bed and flat on my face. Luckily for him, he scooted out of the way before I could land on his back.

"Mmff foo mmff fee omf?"

"I beg your pardon? Mumbling will get you nowhere..." Even with my face to the floor, I could tell he was smirking. Painfully, I lifted my head just enough. He was still on the floor next to me as he'd landed, though now propped up on one elbow.

"Will you help me up?" I repeated, spitting bits of carpet lint out of my mouth. "Please?"

"I should leave you there. Grabbing for my things doesn't earn my trust." He pushed himself up into a sitting position, obviously not about to help me anytime soon.

"...I like roses..." I explained, knowing how pathetic I sounded as soon as the words were out.

"Yes, well...we can't always have what we like...or love..." The smirk was gone from his voice, and I slowly rolled over onto my back. He was now staring down at the rose in his hand, the glitter on the petals resembling a starry sky as it sparkled in the afternoon sunlight beaming through the sliding glass door to the balcony.

"You miss her..."

"Of course...she's never left my mind, even after all these years..."

"I...don't suppose looking at that rose all the time helps any..." I heaved myself up into a sitting position facing him, leaning back against the side of the bed. He studied me for several moments, seemingly perplexed at the amount of details from his past that I knew about. The pain bubbling up from the conversation, however, forced him to silence his questions for a later time.

"No...but that's not why I have it..." He smiled sadly. "Congratulations, you're about to get one of your answers."

"I'm listening..." I gently smiled back.

"I...got it at the gypsy fair I was a part of...They told me it would help me escape to another world...any place or time I could think of, by pressing down on the pearl. I considered using it the night I ran away, but being brought to the Opera House changed that. I kept this rose hidden, first in my stuffed monkey toy, then in a music box I crafted. After...after the one I love left me, I remained in hiding for several days, letting my anger and tears exhaust me enough to the point where I had to either let death take me or fight to make a new life...somewhere my music would finally be heard and appreciated, if I could even manage to make more of it again. Something inside me knew, deep down, that I had to try...It has always brought me such comfort, and so there had to be a reason why.

"So finally I returned to my living quarters to listen to my music box one more time. It was then I remembered the rose, and decided that there wouldn't be a better time than then to use it...start over...and, well...here I am...The rumors about this unit being haunted were already there for me to embrace as I carved out tunnels between buildings and their basements. The stories served me well as both an explanation for the digging sounds as well as a shield of fear against anyone finding those tunnels. It was never in my plan to cause so great a scare that this place would close down, and so when I felt I'd done just enough to protect my new home and to amuse myself, I passed the time by helping with the upkeep, just as I had done back in my world.

"It was after the first couple years when I remembered one thing about this trinket. I'm cursed to remain the same age whenever I use it...until I find someone to love..." The last was said in the most bitter tone that I felt myself tear up along with him. I don't know how I managed it, but the next thing I knew, I had scooted my way over to him. Unable to hug him, I gently leaned in so that my head rested on his shoulder. I felt him stiffen at the contact, and for a moment I thought for sure he'd push me away. Instead, he very slowly wrapped one arm around me, albeit loosely. Even then, he only allowed a few tears and sniffles to escape before he fought against them completely, reaching up to fetch the camera off of the bed behind us. I supposed he needed a distraction, and as he pulled up my previous pictures again, I knew I was right.

Most of them were landscapes of various local scenery, with a few captured sunsets or picturesque clouds. I'd also taken quite a few of woodland critters, mostly in my backyard, as well as several close-ups of the flowering bushes around the resort. "Do you get much chance to spend time outside?" I looked over at him.

"Not nearly as much as you..." He shook his head with the slightest chuckle. "Occasionally, I'll climb up on the roofs...No one ever looks up there..."

"...And...here I thought I was imagining...." I laughed at the realization. "A few times...when I was sweeping off the balconies, I...felt...ever so slightly like I was being watched..."

"And yet you never turned around..." He smirked.

"Even if I had, I bet you would've been able to scoot out of sight..."

"Naturally..." He shrugged before scrolling through to pictures of my calico cat, who I'd been able to take outside with a leash on so that she could enjoy the fresh air without being a danger to my critter friends.

"That's Patches..." I smiled. "She loves you..." At that, he raised an eyebrow, the questions surfacing all over again.

"Whenever I watch the movie, she joins me. By the time 'Music of the Night' comes to an end, she's fallen asleep....and when she's in a grumpy or restless mood, I'll pull up that song to calm her down..."

"So....the trinket at least correctly brought me to a place where my *music* is loved..." He concluded aloud, the bitterness returning. I very nearly addressed the other part he'd been hoping to find, but he never gave me the chance. Straightening back up, he set the camera aside. When I met his gaze, only a slight redness around his unmasked eye gave any trace of his recent emotions. It was as if he'd put on a second invisible mask. "Here's what's going to happen. I will undo your bandages. You will call to go to the hospital as if you'd just regained consciousness from your fall. Once you've healed up, you will request another week's stay because you don't have anything to report. When you return, you will bring your writings about me as well as that movie you mentioned. Once I learn everything you know and feel about me, I will decide what to do with you. Am I clear?"

"I...of course...?" I blinked at his abruptness.

"Good." Silently, he unwrapped all the bandages and carried me down to the master bedroom floor. As soon as the phone was within reach, he disappeared.

****

*******TWO******

The next few weeks passed in a bit of a daze. All I could think about was him and how hard it was for me to not give it all away. I suppose this was my first test of many. The fact that I was excused from work left a bittersweet taste in my mouth. On the one hand, it meant less temptation to spill the beans. On the other, it meant more of a separation from him. I wondered what he was doing...if he was up to his old tricks or if he was moping or just thinking about things. All I knew for sure was I missed him, pranks and all.

When I was mostly recovered, the manager was more than happy to let me try another stay. I suppose she just wanted to get the mystery solved and over with, plus it gave me something to do until I was able to fully resume my duties.

Packing and leaving the house took a little bit longer; I wasn't sure if I'd be back or if he'd keep me prisoner as he'd originally planned. As well as my stories and the movie, I also grabbed extra clothes, some of my most favorite foods and sweets, and a few little gifts for him just to show that I cared. I also hugged my family a little bit longer, including Patches. Now, more than ever, I had the hardest time keeping my mouth shut aside from brave, short 'goodbyes' to each of them.

Finally, I was back in the unit, making myself as at-home as possible. Before I could truly feel settled-in, however, I had to see for myself that he was okay. My coworkers had told me very little upon my return as to what may or may not have occurred in my absence; I reasoned that they were trying to protect me in my recovery. The fact that they were still awaiting a report, though, told me that he'd indeed been up to his old tricks.

As I explored each room, I realized how strangely silent the unit was. Even venturing down into the basement was fruitless; if he were down there, he'd disguised his tunnels so cleverly that it would take me the entirety of the week to find them. *He has to still be here...He wouldn't have used the trinket, would he? He was waiting for my return...* Every step was taken more gingerly than the previous one, rounding every corner of the unit with more caution until I found myself out on the balcony overlooking the golf course through the trees. The singing birds brought a sense of peace to my mind, despite the fact that Erik had still yet to make an appearance. Shrugging off my concern, I decided to fully embrace the moment of fresh air and solitude. Closing my eyes, I took a deep breath and rested my arms on the railing, content to simply listen to the feathered choir.

Just then, I felt something being pressed against my wrists, and I opened my eyes just enough to see my camera balancing on end, being held up by the strap by a hand that wasn't mine. "You never turned around..." His familiarly smirking voice reminded me of my foolishness revealed in our last conversation.

"And spoil your fun? Why would I possibly do that...?" I grinned and spun around. As close as he was, I was very nearly tempted to throw my arms around him, yet I knew he wasn't used to such greetings. Instead, I took my camera from him, thankful he hadn't let me drop it in my shock.

"Foolish curiosity, that's why..." He ignored my sarcasm, his face emotionless save for the slightest betraying sparkle in his eyes. "Now, take those photographs you're wanting." He pointed to the birds before spinning me back around.

"You know me so well..." I giggled, snapping a few shots.

"Not as well as you claim to know me..." He pointed before we both allowed a silence to fall between us. Feeling his eyes on me and now knowing it wasn't just my imagination, I became more self-aware of the amount and quality of pictures I was taking; although he was saying nothing, I knew he had more on his mind besides watching me photograph birds.

"Would you like to try?" I stepped to the side, offering him the camera. He seemed to toy with the idea, his fingers bouncing between extending toward the gadget and clenching into fists of retreat until he dropped his arms to his side.

"Perhaps another time. Did you bring what I asked you to?"

"Of course…" I nodded, turning off the camera. "You mean you want to watch it right now?"

"I thought you said you knew me…!" He raised an eyebrow, tilting his head with the slightest smirk.

"Fair enough…!" I giggled, leading the way downstairs. Unpacking the movie as well as the first of several boxes of tissues, I joined him in the living room where he had already plopped down on the sofa, looking so casually like a king on his throne. Biting my lip at the thought of the impending waves of emotions, I quietly put the movie in before sitting down on the other side of the sofa.

Two and a half hours later, the tissues and the distance between us were gone. I was surprised he'd let me sing along, but the shock was soon lost behind all the other emotions I always went through, no matter how many times I'd watched it. On top of that, here I was sitting next to the man who had experienced it all firsthand, long before I ever knew about him. Yet from the tears now pouring down his face, I could only suspect he'd relived each one of those moments over and over again in his thoughts and sleepless nights ever since.

Another twenty or so minutes passed before he slowly pulled back with a final sniffle. "I...I guess I don't need this around you then..." He reached up towards his mask.

"Whatever makes you comfortable, Erik..." I placed my hand on his.

"It needs to be done sooner or later...Best you get used to it completely." He didn't look at me as he placed the mask on the coffee table. I hesitated for several minutes, watching for any cues. He gave me none.

"M–may I...?" I finally broke the silence. A few moments went by before he slowly nodded. Ever so gently, I reached a shaky hand toward his face. I'd dreamed of this...written about it so often...I wanted it done right. Carefully tracing each scar and bump, I watched as he closed his eyes, tearing up all over again. "I–I'm sorry, Erik...I'm sorry that I'm not her...and that you've been left in so much pain..." He finally met my own tearful gaze, and quite some time passed while we tried to determine who was supposed to be the strong one here. Finally, we realized neither of us could be it. Wrapping our arms around each other, we wept together once again.

When our tears were spent, I slowly pulled back and took a deep breath. "I'm going to make brownies...we both need some cheering up..."

"...Brownies? You mean...those little squares of chocolate cake...?" His eyes widened.

"Yes...have you had them before?" As I stood up, he frowned and shook his head.

"They were always making them...filling the unit with the aroma...never leaving a crumb..."

"Oh, I know the feeling!" I giggled. "Want to watch? I'll let you lick the bowl and have the first one—" That was all I could get out before a caped blur shot past me into the kitchen, already setting out the mixing bowl, measuring utensils, and whisk. I recovered fairly quickly, getting the pan ready and the ingredients out of the cupboard and fridge. In no time at all, Erik was tasting his very first finger-full of brownie batter. Before I could ask what he thought of it, he grabbed the bowl and started for the stairs. I pounced just in time, grabbing his arm. "Not so fast!"

"Mademoiselle, are you trying to injure yourself again?" He raised an eyebrow, taking a second and third taste of batter.

"Well if you behaved, I wouldn't have to risk it, now, would I?" I grabbed the bowl back. A tug-of-war ensued, resulting in us both thunking to the floor, licking brownie batter off of our arms and hands as the metal bowl spun wildly across the kitchen floor. Batter was spraying everywhere in a housekeeping nightmare, but at the moment, I did not care!

"This is all well and good, but you still owe me my first brownie..." He stood up. "Cooked..." he added with a chuckle.

"And suppose that was my only box of mix..." I crossed my arms in mock defiance.

"Nice try. I already counted..." He called my bluff, pulling me to my feet by my still-crossed arms.

"Cheater..." I stuck my tongue out at him before retrieving the bowl.

Amazingly, it was still halfway filled with untouched batter, and so when I finally pulled the pan out of the oven, the brownies were extra thick. Before he could even think of reaching for one, I planted myself firmly between him and the stove. "They have to cool first..."

"Nonsense!" He glared, reaching around me. A fairly loud yelp followed, complete with him racing to the freezer to stick his hand in.

"You really should learn to trust me, Erik..." I stifled a giggle, getting some aloe gel out of one of my bags. "Why don't you take my stories into one of the bedrooms? I'll bring you your brownie when they're ready." As I gently applied the cooling gel to his hand, he sighed in resignation. I could tell his pride was more scorched than anything else of his, and I knew he needed some time alone. Sure enough, he was silent as he gathered up my notebooks and trudged upstairs.

****

The unit was quiet...too quiet as I made my way up with his brownie, a glass of milk, and a plate of shrimp and broccoli alfredo. I found him hunched over the desk in the loft, papers and notebooks scattered in front of him and all across the beds on either side of him. "Are...they that awful...?" I bit my lip.

"Your talent is not the issue, Mademoiselle..." He slowly glanced over at me. "It's that ridiculous imagination..."

"I tried to keep it realistic..." I brought his supper over and set it down.

"How could you possibly think that anyone could love me?" He shoved one of the stories into my hands.

"It's very simple, Erik. Everyone deserves to be loved..."

"She didn't think so. Even in all those stories, you could have changed her mind...Not once did you have her love me!"

"Erik, even if I had...it doesn't change the fact. It doesn't change your world...in the end, they're only stories..." I sat down on one of the beds, placing a hand on his arm. "I think...I think she wanted to love you...just not in the way you hoped. She loved you as a father figure...teacher...friend...When she gave you that ring...it was like she was giving you the chance to love someone else..."

"Well that's out of the question." He pulled his arm out of my grasp, standing up. "I'm...grateful for your good intentions, Sarah...but I'm afraid you wasted your time and talent. My heart will always belong to her, and her alone. It's best if you get that through your head right now." I almost wanted to tell him that I'd never stop hoping for happiness for him, but one look at his face told me to keep silent. Slowly gathering up the stories, I returned downstairs.

****

I didn't hear from him at all the rest of the night, and he remained upstairs through the entirety of the next day. As much as I tried to relax, even treating myself to a bubble bath and random rom-com movie that happened to be on, he never left my mind. All I could think of was how I'd certainly broken his heart all over again, and I had no idea how to help. This wasn't another one of my stories where a few strokes of the pen could fix everything. This was real. His need for space was evident, however, by his continued absence, and so I fought back every urge to check on him. I did make enough of each meal so that he could help himself to the leftovers if he felt up to it, choosing fragrant dishes that would alert his stomach once he smelled them cooking.

That second night, a thunderstorm overhead woke me just enough to hear Erik in the kitchen, the unmistakable crinkle of foil betraying his need for another brownie. I smiled to myself, feeling a little more at peace knowing he was at least eating. It seemed as though I continued to drift in and out of sleep between every clap of thunder or flicker of lightning, not knowing if I was dreaming or if I was really hearing Erik pacing or wandering through the unit. I tried to shove it all to the back of my mind and get the sleep I was needing, but was then fully awakened by an exceptionally bright burst of lightning followed by the sound of the basement door closing. I glanced toward the alarm clock, but its blank darkness indicated that the power had been knocked out. *Lovely*...I sighed, sliding out of bed and into my slippers.

For the most part, I had the layout of the unit memorized; it was only after crossing the hallway to the basement door that I began having issues with the lack of light. As soon as I set foot on the narrow ladder only meant for the occasional maintenance man access, my own foolishness dawned on me. The only other time I'd been down there was two days prior, during daylight and with the aid of the overhead light bulbs. Even then, I hadn't been able to find the entrance to his tunnels. Still, something almost instinctual forced me to continue down the ladder.

Just then, my hand brushed against a thick spider web as eight tiny legs scrambled over my knuckles. "YiiiiEEEEE!" I yanked my hand away, stupidly letting go completely to brush at it with my other hand. Before I could totally lose my balance, however, firm hands pressed into my back, steadying me.

"Sarah, what on earth...??" Erik hissed. "Are you trying to get injured all over again??"

"N–no....just...couldn't sleep..." I mumbled, not even trying to make it sound better than the half-truth it was. Heaving a sigh, he gently helped me down the rest of the ladder.

"It's only a common thunderstorm, Mademoiselle...Surely you've endured them before..."

"It wasn't that..." I shook my head, not caring if he could see the motion or not. "The storm only heightened what was already going through my mind..."

"Thus, 'Music of the Night' was born..." His voice was distant, but only for a moment. "I understand all too well, but there is nothing you need concern yourself with that cannot wait til morning. Right now, it's best you return to your bed."

"I'm too awake now..." I realized out loud. "...Unless, you were on *your* way to bed...I would hate to keep you up..." At that, he let out a low chuckle.

"No, dear writer, you yourself figured out within your stories that I do not sleep unless sleep finds me. And you know all too well, oddly enough, the reasoning for that."

"So it is true...the nightmares and flashbacks..."

"I need no reminder." He growled.

"How about company then...?" I offered, part of me dreading the climb back up the ladder and finding yet another spider home.

"I suppose, for a moment..." He agreed a little too quickly, his voice heavy with sadness I couldn't quite comprehend.

"Sounds like I'm not the only one whose mind is cluttered tonight..." I attempted to open the door of conversation. When he did finally speak after a brief pause, however, he chose to ignore the listening ear I was offering.

"Come...we'll go to the tunnels where we can at least sit in my living quarters. I won't force you back up the ladder just yet. Clearly you and climbing in dark spaces are sworn enemies..." He managed a chuckle through whatever was troubling him.

"How considerate of you..." I retorted with thick sarcasm. He was silent as he guided me along the walls, stopping at what felt like a set of shelves. I heard something click, and then the shelves creaked aside, cool damp air making contact with my face.

"Wow..." I breathed with a shiver; although all I could see was more darkness ahead, my imagination was running wild with the possibilities of what I could be staring at. Erik's story aside, I'd always been intrigued by secret passageways, and now I was finally experiencing one.

"It's merely a tunnel, Mademoiselle...not nearly as advanced as I had at the Opera House..."

"Still, it's something you made...I imagine it took quite a great deal of time and effort..."

"Time was all I had..." His voice was distant again, but he remained close, prodding me to go ahead of him. He brought my hand up so that I could feel my way along the walls as we went. I pushed my questions to the back of my mind, certain he'd reveal his reasoning for it in due time.

After countless steps in complete silence, he stopped me in front of a thick piece of cloth that felt suspiciously like one of the dining room drapes. "Wait here..." He instructed, moving aside the curtain so that he could pass through ahead of me. The sudden solitude woke my imagination all the more as my hands began to tingle with spiderweb memories. The more I peered into the darkness, the darker it seemed to get, and so I squeezed my eyes shut. Just then, his hand reached out and pulled me past the curtain, where all at once a bit of brightness warmed my eyelids, beckoning them open.

The room seemed to be more storage space than living quarters as he had managed to rescue quite a few pieces of furniture and decor over the years he'd been here. The source of light was an odd blend of modern electric lanterns, scented candles, and timeless taper candles. Pieces of carpeting were scattered all over the floor while the walls were draped in sheets and blankets that made it feel more like a tent. The amount of framed artwork could have defined the room as a gallery, yet central to the space was a king-size bed, frame and all, as well as a desk and several chairs in various stages of repair. Books were piled everywhere as shelving seemed to be limited. "You really have been busy..." I continued to take it all in.

"Artwork should never be discarded for destruction..." He replied a little more harshly than I suspect he intended, and then his voice softened as if remembering who he was talking to. "Each of these items was crafted by someone...the pictures, the linens, the furniture...the books..." He glanced at me then before continuing. "I intended to bring life back to them all..."

"...You...mean *intend*, right...? Present tense...?" He didn't answer me right away, busying himself with turning down the blankets on the bed and fluffing up the pillow. "...Erik...?"

"I set this bed up for you, with the mindset that you would stay down here as my prisoner. It's yours, so you might as well sleep here tonight. I hope you were paying attention when I led you here, because I won't be able to guide you back. Finish your week's stay, Mademoiselle...When you write your report, just say that this place won't be bothered by me any longer."

"Erik..." I made my way over to him. "...I didn't mean to ruin your fun...I didn't want to take any joy away from you...You don't have to go..."

"Yes, I think I do..." He slowly reached into his pocket. When I saw him pull out the rose trinket, my eyes widened.

"Where will you go?"

"I might as well return to my world..." he sighed, "There's nothing for me anywhere else. Besides, I must be there to leave a rose on Christine's grave..."

"But...I'll miss you..." Tears splashed down my face before I could stop them. "I know now that you're more than just a character I like...You're a real man...a real human being with feelings and longings...Someone whose friendship I almost had before I ruined it all...a—and if you leave..." I stumbled closer, not caring about how dramatic I was being.

"You ruined nothing, Sarah..." He placed a steadying hand on my shoulder. "Only learned that my heartbreak and bitterness are more permanent than you thought, although your insight into my mind and heart is...remarkable, almost unsettling. I cannot figure out how someone such as yourself, who finds joy in just about everything, could be so knowledgeable and understanding of my darkness as if you had experienced it yourself. I even borrowed your camera while you were bathing...I took it up to the roof to try to look at the world through your eyes, but all I could capture was the coming storm clouds.

"Don't you see? If anything, I ruined your hopes for me. And so perhaps it's best that I leave. You shouldn't stop writing...I shouldn't stand in your way...Keep that light of yours shining. I'm only sorry my darkness is too much for you...I'm too far gone..." With a final touch to my face, he stepped back, placing his thumb over the pearl center of the trinket. There was no time to think or decide. At the last possible second, I leapt forward, grasping his hands.

****

****THREE****

With a shiver, I opened my eyes. Snow was falling onto my face. I sat up, noticing Erik glaring at me a few feet away. "What did you do that for? There are consequences...What were you thinking, woman?"

"I...wasn't about to say good bye...not like that..." I pulled my knees up to my chest.

"Yes, well...if you remember correctly, I didn't exactly utter those words either..." He looked away.

"We're...not in your lair..." I observed, and he let out a bitter chuckle.

"I...had her on my mind...We're outside their house..."

"I...I see..." I bit my lip, partly to keep it from trembling.

"It's Christmas here...I've been hearing laughter and some traditional music from inside..." He made no motion towards me, let alone any acknowledgement of my shivering.

"Do you want to take a look...?" I attempted to delicately hurry us along. The sooner he got his bearings and satisfied his curiosity, we could decide where to go from here. Preferably someplace warm.

"A quick one..." He slowly nodded. "I cannot bear anything more than that." Silently, he pushed himself up, peering into the window but not moving any closer. Not wasting any time, I joined him and saw that, by now, Christine and Raoul were parents to two beautiful girls, and a third child on the way. The oldest girl looked to be about five, and I threw a questioning glance at Erik. Although he was paying me no mind whatsoever, he seemingly read my thoughts. "I was in your world for six years. It would appear that the same amount of time passed here...perhaps a few months more, given the season. She's...so happy...She's forgotten me...just as I told her to. She...always did listen to me well..."

"I very much doubt she's forgotten you entirely, Erik..." I lightly touched his arm, resisting the urge to hide my hand inside his warm cape. "You added so much to her life. You were the father figure, teacher, and friend that she needed. You gave her her voice back..."

"Yes, and look how she repaid me!" He glared, moving away from me.

"The ring, Erik...It was originally and rightfully hers to keep. But she gave it to you. She believed in you just as much as you believed in her!"

"No...She had potential I never will. As I said, to love anyone but her would be impossible for me....let alone anyone loving me in return..." Before I could continue the argument, the front door swung open, and there she was, staring out at us in bewilderment.

"Angel...?" She finally managed, only to be answered with silence. "You...must be freezing...won't you come inside?" I think if I hadn't been there to pull his arm, he would indeed have frozen, the look of a deer in the headlights forever on his face. Blankets were thrown around us before we were led to the sofa by the fireplace. His eyes never left her, but he did manage to hide his scars from the two girls' curious stares. Raoul entered the room behind his wife.

"Christine...?" his eyes locked on his rival.

"Don't start...It's Christmas..." Christine glanced back at him stubbornly.

"I...suppose I can't argue with that..." He sighed. "Marguerite? Lottie? Best run upstairs now and get ready for dinner. It'll be served in about an hour." He threw me a questioning glance as he ushered the girls out of the room, and I realized my outfit was the cause of such a look. In a plain t-shirt and floral pajama bottoms, I wasn't just underdressed for the season, but also very obviously not a local. Christine seemed to sense this and smiled warmly.

"Come with me...I'm sure I'll have something a little more...suitable..." She then looked at Erik. "You...will stay, won't you?"

"Only as long as you wish..." he managed. Confident that he wouldn't disappear, we made our way upstairs.

"Forgive me, I lost my manners in my shock...I'm Christine..."

"Sarah...There's no need to apologize. I...Erik's told me so much about you..."

"I'm sure he has..." She opened her wardrobe doors. "You must tell me how and where you met!"

"Oh..! Well, he's been...traveling all this time...We met at a...hotel in America..." I replied truthfully.

"How fascinating! Peculiar though, that he would bring his lady friend to the home of his first love for Christmas...And he didn't prepare you for the weather...?"

"I...this visit was fairly last-minute...I sort of invited myself along..." I was grateful when the amount of dresses she set out for me to choose from served as a seamless change-of-subject. "They're so beautiful! I couldn't possibly..."

"Nonsense! We normally only wear each dress once anyway...I'm more than happy to see them get more use!" She grinned, holding up a simple yet elegant gown of blue and white. "Yes...this will do...I'm sure you'll be wanting a hot bath first?"

"No need to trouble yourself..."

"It's no trouble at all!" And then, before I could protest further, her maids were filling the room, pampering me more than

I could have begun to imagine. By the time I finally descended the staircase, I felt like and certainly looked like a brand new person, born and raised in 19th century Paris.

As I neared the bottom step, I could hear some giggling from over by the fireplace. When I entered the sitting room, I had to stifle my own giggle. "No, Monsieur, you hold it like this!" Little Lottie fixed Erik's grip around a tiny porcelain teacup from her apparently gifted set while her older sister covered her mouth. The three of them were crowded around the coffee table, Erik still wrapped in his blanket and looking very much trapped. Not wanting to interrupt, I quietly lowered myself to the nearest chair to the doorway.

"Would you care for another pastry?" Marguerite continued the impromptu table manners lesson, holding an empty plate out to him.

"No...thank you...I'm...perfectly satisfied..." He stammered.

"More tea then?" Lottie looked up at him with the most adorable eyes. So wide-eyed was she that rather than reminding her that she'd only just filled his cup seconds earlier, he simply nodded.

"Oh!!" Marguerite cried with such suddenness that Erik had to scramble to catch his cup before anything 'spilled' or shattered. "I've forgotten the sugar! You must think me a terrible hostess!"

"Th–that's...perfectly alright...I don't need any–" But before Erik could finish consoling the girl, she plopped three imaginary cubes into his cup.

"Now, Marguerite, a good hostess listens to her guests' preferences..." Christine's voice sounded from the doorway behind me, and Erik paled upon realization that he had an audience. "Have you warmed yourself sufficiently, Angel?" She ignored his obvious panic.

"Yes...thank you..." He slowly unfolded himself from the uncomfortable position on the floor, draping his blanket over the back of a chair.

"You're most welcome...Girls, put your tea set away now. Dinner's ready..." Taking both daughters by the hand, she led the way into the dining room where her husband was waiting to seat her. He still looked less than pleased with Erik's presence, but I could tell his compliance to his wife's wishes was out of sheer love for her. Yes, as they exchanged smiles, I knew theirs was the truest of loves...a love I could only hope for for Erik, and for myself.

Erik and I were seated at the opposite end of the table from the couple, the girls in between. Thankfully, their excited chatter over the holiday and tea party took away the awkward silence that most definitely would have taken place in their absence. Without looking at him, I could feel how hard it was for Erik to be here. On the other hand, I hoped he was thinking and asking himself if he really wanted to take Christine away from all this happiness.

****

Although Christine persuaded her husband to invite us to stay the night, Erik understandably declined. We'd learned that the Girys had moved to the countryside further northwest from Paris than the DeChagney estate, and that Meg was now engaged to a wood carver. I wondered if Erik was going to try to see them tonight, but instead he aimed for the city lights. It was quite a while before I dared to speak. "The...girls seemed to like you..." At that, he scoffed.

"They dragged me to the floor, Sarah! I thought keeping someone prisoner was a *poor* sign of admiration..."

"They're little girls...they'll learn in time..."

"Hopefully not the hard way..."

"Ah, so you like them too..." I pointed.

"I wouldn't wish my pain on *anyone*, Mademoiselle. Besides, their eyes were too big to argue with."

"Yes, of course..." I hid my smile. "So...I'm guessing we're going to the Opera House...?"

"*I* am Mademoiselle. You, on the other hand, are returning to your world." He reached into his pocket and pulled out the trinket. "Now then...this has one trip left in it, and then you may keep it to remember me by. But you should be with your family....those who love you. I have nothing to offer except an eternity of darkness, and now neither one of us can age. But at least you stand a chance in your world..."

"Won't you come with me?" I felt my lower lip begin to tremble, only this time, it wasn't from the cold.

"As I said, I must be here to leave that rose and ring." He touched my shoulder with one hand while pressing the trinket into mine with the other.

"I'm not leaving without you, Erik...That time away recovering...it was torture...!" I sniffled.

"You're only making this harder for yourself! You'll survive!"

"But will you? Can you honestly say you'll be okay with an eternity of loneliness? Look me in the eyes and tell me that truthfully, and I'll go."

"Sarah, stop being stubborn!" He gently shoved me away, not meeting my gaze. "I told you, I'm a waste of your time! Now go! Think of home, and go!" He was using the very same tone and volume that he did after Christine's kiss. At that moment, my decision was made. Through the blur of tears, I watched him start walking away again. And then, I pressed the pearl.

****

As I woke up the next morning, I could hear the distant sound of someone approaching. I quietly climbed out of bed, moving to a chair to wait. A few minutes later, the boat moved under the raised gate, and there he was. He didn't see me at first. Not until he pulled the boat onto the rocky shore and stumbled toward the bedroom did his gaze finally fall on me. And he wasn't happy. "You...."

"I used the trinket. The magic is gone. I'm staying."

"You **insolent**..." He growled, then let out an exasperated sigh. "Why will you not listen to me? And you want me to trust you?"

"You didn't say it, Erik...With all your masks and disguises, you couldn't even lie about being okay on your own. I only lived up to my word." I hated to say it. I hated making him angrier than he already was. But it was the truth.

"What do you want from me?" He shoved a candelabra into the water.

"Nothing. Absolutely nothing. Just...no more goodbyes..." He studied me for several minutes before sighing again.

"Very well. We won't say goodbye. We won't speak a single word to each other. You insist on staying, then you will stay in complete silence. The bedroom is yours...you'll go nowhere else. Am I clear?" I could only nod in response, returning to the massive bed...So beautiful a piece of furniture, and now it was to be my prison. I wouldn't cry. I asked for this. In time, I was sure he'd change his mind.

****

****FOUR****

For the next few months or so(I lost track of time fairly easily in the darkness), his vow of silence held. He wasn't cruel, however. He provided food and drink on a regular basis, plated on the steps but not covered, and so I had to pay attention if I wanted my meal hot and fresh. Every once in a while, he'd even shove a tub of hot water onto the bedroom platform, and, after dropping a towel and chunk of soap beside it, he'd disappear into one of his many other caverns to give me privacy. Once, he surprised me with a new black dress; seemingly made from one of his extra capes. I concluded it wasn't meant as a gift, however. My blue and white gown surely only reminded him of who I got it from.

Mostly, however, he kept to himself, gradually taking care of what had been damaged by the mob. The music box was the first item he tended to, stitching up a few rips before solemnly giving it a seat of honor on the back of the organ, not allowing a single note to play from either. The broken glass from the mirrors was swept into a pile; several times, he'd revisit that pile, picking up a few pieces to examine before tossing them back down to the floor out of frustration. He would then move on to a simpler task, such as repairing pieces of furniture or returning artwork to their rightful places.

To occupy myself in between meals, baths, and watching him work, I took it upon myself to keep my own area clean. It helped me to remember my world and my housekeeping training. I could have written a thousand stories, surrounded by inspiration, but somehow it didn't feel right. Instead, I read books from the smaller of his two collections; the larger one was in his work room, convenient for any research needed.

So lost was I in one particular volume that I didn't notice him sit down on the foot of the bed until he cleared his throat. It's a wonder the book didn't end up flying through the air and plopping into the lake. Instead, it landed square in the middle of his lap. "....sorry..." I bit my lip.

"...Mademoiselle. *Aesop's Fables* are hardly suspenseful to begin with, but you've read that ten times now. There's no cause for you to be so jumpy." He calmly closed the book and set it aside.

"I...guess I've simply grown used to the silence..." I smiled sheepishly.

"That makes two of us...Even if I still think you a fool, I've...grown accustomed to your company. Insanity and all." He lowered his gaze to his hands. "All this time of accusing you of breaking my trust, I should have been realizing how much *you* trust *me*...even though everything I've done speaks volumes of why you shouldn't..."

"Erik, everyone's got something about themselves that they aren't proud of...There's no such thing as a perfect human being. Besides...I believe in a loving, forgiving God. If He can forgive the sins of the world to the point of dying on the cross for each and every one...who am I to hold anything against you?"

"Yes, I've read through the Bible, Sarah...I still don't understand how or why..."

"Could you bring it over?" Silently, he fetched it from his work room, and I flipped through the pages to Psalm a-hundred-and-thirty-nine. Reading through the verses, I glanced up at him. "You're His creation, Erik...His work of art. Just like you cherish each of your drawings and paintings, so does He cherish you. We're not supposed to fully understand...Just accept it."

"But I disobeyed Him...turned my back on Him..." This prompted me to tell him about the prodigal son.

"He knows we're not perfect. He didn't create puppets. He gave us the freedom to choose because forced love isn't true love."

"Just like I could never force Christine to love me..." he sighed.

"Exactly. And, Erik, I do know your pain. I've loved and lost before. I didn't realize it then, but I realize now that it was the wrong kind of love...it was a blinding love that caused me to do some very wrong things...I was selfish and so in love with being in love and having a boyfriend that I didn't want to jeopardize it. So I said yes countless times when I should have said no...And for a while after we parted ways, the guilt just overwhelmed me. That's when God reminded me of His Promise and Presence...His Love and forgiveness...I now have a second chance, and now I can use it for His Glory."

"You've...been wanting to tell me this for a while, haven't you...?" He was struggling to keep his voice steady.

"Of course. That's why I wrote all those stories, Erik...I want you to find the truest form of happiness and inner peace..."

"How can I?? Without her...Without hope..."

"There's always hope, Erik. You sell yourself far too short. And it is possible...You just need to learn not to depend on anyone else for your happiness. If you truly love her, which I know you do, don't put that pressure on her shoulders. Don't try to steal her happiness." That did it. With a single sniffle, his head fell into my arms. The caverns then fell silent aside from his whimpers and sobs, and I took that time to pray for guidance for myself and healing for his heart.

"How long did it take you to move on, Sarah?" The question came about an hour later, after his tears were spent but when he was still too emotionally exhausted to pull away from my arms.

"Honestly? A matter of years...I felt like I couldn't be that happy again without him, and if I really thought about it, I would have said I didn't *want* to be happy without him. I guess I figured if I was, it would make what we had less special or significant. But God eventually showed me that such a mindset was only killing me inside. It wasn't healthy...and I didn't want to spend the rest of my life dwelling on it."

"...I feel another comparison to my situation coming on..." he let the slightest chuckle escape.

"You're beginning to know me too well..." I smiled back. "It's true though...You can choose to spend eternity in lonely darkness, or you can choose to give the outside world a chance to really get to know the real you..."

"You really believe there's someone out there for me?"

"You'll never find out sulking down here..."

"I suppose you're right..." he sighed.

"But first, you've got to focus on your own heart...letting God fill it with His love so that you can love others. Then, in time, when He sees fit, He'll show her to you."

"I'm scared..." They were two words, but they were heavy with vulnerability. I remembered writing about *him* being the wandering child, and now I could see in his eyes how true that was. Absentmindedly holding him closer, I smiled gently.

"That's why I stayed, Erik...You're not alone. I want to help you..."

"I don't have any more tears to shed..."

"...sorry..." I smiled a bit more. "If I had the ingredients, I'd whip up some more brownies..." At that, he finally chuckled.

"The market will have a variety of pastries..." He thought a bit before retrieving a small stack of bills from a nearby chest. "You should get some fresh air...Go, treat yourself to anything you'd like for your stay down here..."

"Are you sure?"

"You're no longer my prisoner, Sarah...You never were. I could never hold you here, and even if I were, I trust you...." He pressed the money into my hands. After he showed me the way out, I looked at him.

"You should get some sleep..."

"I'll try..." He slowly nodded. "Now go ahead and spoil yourself." With a final smile, he turned around and headed back into the tunnels.

****

The early spring weather seemed to be drawing every Parisian out of hibernation. Swept up in the crowds, I easily lost track of time. He'd told me to spoil myself, but I picked up several things for him as well, along with a basket of pastries to share. The sun was almost fully set before I returned to the Opera House, struggling to balance the armload of parcels as well as see around them all. It's a wonder I didn't stumble or trip into the lake, but it seemed like the packages knew right when I was back in the lair; at the very last second, they went thunking to the floor. They're lucky none of them were fragile and that Erik had fallen into a deep sleep. I couldn't help but smile at the picture of him curled up in a tight ball on the bed, his hands seeming to be clutching something. Rather than prying, I carefully pulled the blanket up around him before busying myself with the purchases.

By the time I heard him stir, I'd managed to hang some curtains around the bedroom to section it off. My new dresses were folded and put away along with my new books. The pastries were brought into the kitchen cavern, and while supper was cooking, I set my gifts for him out on his work tables. They were practical, but the fanciest I could afford; a drawing and writing utensil set, new gloves, and a new cloak. The last gift wasn't quite as practical, but I couldn't resist it—a companion for his stuffed monkey from his childhood. I was looking for the perfect spot for it when he finally woke up. "Supper smells good..." he mumbled drowsily.

"I hope so..." I smiled and brought him the monkey. "I thought maybe your monkey could use a friend as well..."

"You...is this a gift...? For me...?" He blinked.

"Now don't start that again..." I giggled and handed it to him. "I would have given you some back in my world, but the opportunity never presented itself. Besides...Christmas went by and I didn't get you a thing for it..."

"I...I see..." He studied the monkey a bit before reaching into his pocket. "That being the case...I was going to save this...as a thank you..." He then stepped behind me, draping a necklace over my head. Looking down, I noticed he'd fashioned the rose trinket into a pendant.

"Oh my, Erik, is there any talent you don't have?" I blinked back my own tears.

"Dancing..." He shrugged jokingly, and I hugged him tightly.

"Thank you..."

"Thank *you*, Sarah...For your friendship...for putting up with my moods...In all honesty, when I first saw you had come here...I wasn't simply angry at your disobedience. That was part of it, of course, but...I had spent the entire night's walk back to the Opera House fighting within myself. I didn't want to surrender to the thought of never seeing you again...missing you...I had finally let you go by the time I got here...and then, seeing you...I was frustrated that my inward debate had been for nothing...except now there would most likely be another instance where I'll have to let you go all over again..."

"Well that won't be anytime soon, if I have anything to say about it...!" I gave his hand a squeeze. "Now, how about we see about supper? There are plenty of pastries to choose from for dessert..!"

"If supper didn't smell so appetizing, I'd skip to dessert entirely..!" He chuckled, leading the way into the kitchen.

****

As the next couple of months passed, our friendship grew stronger. He helped me start keeping track of the days by requesting a Bible study session each evening, where we would take turns reading different passages and I would answer his questions as best as I could. Each of these sessions would end with me praying for continued wisdom and guidance for us both, until one night, he began praying instead. It brought me such warmth and joy to hear his candid, childlike conversations with the Heavenly Father that we shared, now that he had acknowledged his need for Jesus and believed fully in the message of the cross.

Over the course of a few days scattered here and there, he gradually gave me a full tour of his caverns, and I was shocked to see my artistic guesses hadn't been very far from the truth. Most of the hidden caves were empty, but a few served as storage for more than twenty years' worth of clothes, costumes, furnishings, decor, instruments, and masks. "Do you play?" he motioned one day to a collection of stringed instruments.

"No...I sing though...not well enough for the opera, as you heard when we watched the movie..." He was quiet then, as if debating with himself as to whether or not he was ready to train anyone after Christine.

"Perhaps someday..." he concluded aloud. I went over and picked up a violin.

"How long has it been?"

"Too long..." He started to reach for it, but stopped. "And yet perhaps not long enough...I don't know if I can..."

"You won't know until you try, Erik..." I handed it to him before sitting down against the cavern wall. I watched as he carefully tuned the old instrument, almost purposely taking his own sweet time. "Ask Him to give you a song..." I pointed upward, and he took a deep breath. Closing his eyes, he moved the bow across the strings in an aimless but heartfelt tune.

So lost in the music were we both that the approaching footsteps went unnoticed. "Well! Even after Christine told us, I wouldn't believe it until I saw for myself...Welcome back, Erik..!" Antoinette Giry entered the room, tears streaming down her face.

"Antoinette...!" Erik nearly dropped the violin. "How–you've never crossed the lake before..!"

"I followed the music..." She explained simply. "I...I came to invite you to Meg's wedding next month."

"I...don't know what to say..." Erik stammered, and Antoinette took that moment to acknowledge me.

"You must be Sarah...Christine told me so much about your Christmas visit. Your presence seems to have worked wonders on Erik..."

"All I did was what anyone would do for a friend..." I smiled shyly.

"Well it's just what he needed then." She returned the smile. "I hope you both visit before the wedding. My daughter could use the company, and Christine can only do so much with her new baby arriving any day now."

"Of course!" I replied hastily, before realizing I should have asked Erik his preference.

"Wonderful!" She jotted down a few directions.

"Can I get you anything before you go back?"

"Perhaps some tea..." The older woman nodded, and we left Erik to collect his thoughts.

Madame Giry left a few hours later, and even then, Erik didn't emerge from the back caverns until his supper had gone cold. "I'm sorry, Erik, if I spoke out of turn..." I couldn't help but notice his emotionless expression.

"You didn't...I mean...I figure you were caught up in the excitement. After all, it's high time you got some female company..." He sat down heavily in his chair then, moving the food around aimlessly in his dish.

"I could warm that up for you..." I bit my lip, trying to read him.

"No...it's fine..."

"Erik, what is it...?" I moved my chair a bit closer.

"Are you truly happy here, Sarah?" He looked over at me.

"Of course I am..!" I gently took his hand.

"Be honest...You miss your friends...your family..."

"I do...But I don't regret what I did..."

"You're not just saying that because you can't change your mind?"

"Erik, for goodness sake!" I let out an exasperated sigh. "Where is all this coming from?"

"You deserve more than me, Sarah...More than this life...this darkness...You won't find the right man for you if you keep hiding down here..."

"I don't care about that, Erik. I care about *you*!" He studied me for several minutes before sighing, taking a bite of food.

"I just don't want you to be blinded, Sarah...You're...very kind...very sweet...I don't want to take advantage of that or for you to be made to feel naive..."

"Then stop talking like this..." I offered a small smile. "I knew perfectly well what I was doing when I came here. You're a wonderful man...a great friend. I enjoy your company very much. As you even said, I've never been your prisoner. This was my choice." Giving his hand a squeeze, I jumped up to get him a pastry before too many of his tears could fall. Two seconds after leaving the room, it dawned on me. "...It's because I was in such a rush to have tea with Madame Giry that I completely left you in the dust, isn't it...?"

"Perhaps..." He sniffed.

"Oh, Erik...!" I giggled and hugged his pout away.

****

****FIVE****

Our visit to the Giry cottage took place about a week later. Erik decided not to send word ahead of time, as he was still wary of interacting with those from his past, especially in too formal a social setting. "She'll make a fuss. It's better this way." he'd given a final nod before closing the subject. He opted to rent a carriage rather than walk or hire a driver, and when we pulled up to the little house, we were slightly surprised to see a second one already parked in front of the stables, with the driver dozing inside. "Company..." Erik muttered, looking ready to turn right around and change his mind about the whole thing.

"We're already here..." I pointed softly. "It could be Meg's fiance...in which case you'd be meeting him soon anyway."

"I wish you'd quit this nonsense of being so right all the time." He growled with a relenting sigh. He barely remembered to help me down, staring at the front door while adjusting his cloak hood around his face. Not giving him a chance to have second thoughts, I gently pulled him to the door and knocked. It was opened promptly by Meg, who didn't seem to notice me as she stared wide-eyed at Erik.

"You're here..."

"Yes, Little Giry...The Phantom of the Opera..." Erik's voice was playful, yet shaky. She threw her arms around him then as if welcoming home a long lost brother or cousin.

"I'm so glad! Mama said you might, but neither of us wanted to get our hopes up..." She then finally took notice of me, hesitating a few seconds before pulling me into a hug. "After what Mama told me about you, I couldn't wait to meet you!"

"And I you!" I smiled, returning the hug. "Congratulations on your engagement..!"

"Thank you!" Her grin widened as she led us into the sitting room. At that moment, we all froze. Seated on the sofa next to Antoinette was Christine. "O–oh dear...I..." Meg bit her lip apologetically, looking nervously between Erik and the Vicomtesse.

"Never you mind, my child..." Antoinette spoke up. "All are welcome in this house at any time. I'll bring some more tea." She patted Christine's hand before rising to her feet. "Erik? Sarah, do make yourselves comfortable..." She flashed an unreadable but stern look toward Erik before disappearing into the kitchen. He seemed to understand it immediately, though, as he lowered himself to a chair across the coffee table from Christine. I took a seat between him and Meg.

"It's nice to see you again..." I smiled at Christine, hoping to distract them both from the awkwardness of the situation. "You're looking well..."

"Thank you...I certainly don't feel it, but the discomfort will be over soon enough." She returned the smile gratefully, shifting her position slightly. "My hus–Raoul," she glanced at Erik, choosing to soften the blow of her words, "thought I should spend the afternoon here, to get my mind off of things as well as give me a bit of a break from the girls..."

"She also wanted to get as many wedding plans worked out for me as possible before the new baby arrives..." Meg pointed. "Mama and I won't let her do much though!"

"Meg, I told you I'm fine!" Christine rolled her eyes with a giggle.

"Yes, and we're going to make sure you *stay* fine!" Meg made a face at her, and I felt the slightest pang of sadness, reminded of the banter I no longer would have with my friends and siblings.

"You truly are happy..." Erik's mumble interrupted my silent pity party, shocking all of us, including himself.

"I..really am...Erik..." Christine's eyes watered as she addressed him by name for the first time. "My choice has made me very happy....but...you'll always hold a very special place with me...I figure, we were both exactly what the other needed at the time...nothing more, but certainly nothing less...I owe a great deal to you, truly..."

"No...just keep being happy, Christine. That's all I—" Erik stopped himself, slowly standing up.

"Don't go..." Meg jumped up as well, grasping his hand. "Please..."

"I..just need to...I'll see if your mother needs help..." He managed a tight smile, which satisfied us all as we watched him head towards the kitchen. Our conversation soon turned to the upcoming wedding, and I was fascinated to hear about the traditions as well as the personalized ideas, some inspiration of which was carried over from the DeChagneys' wedding. It seemed as though they were about to ask me about weddings where I was from, when all of a sudden Christine's face took on a pained expression.

"O–oh...!" she gasped, gripping the sofa cushion on either side of her.

"...Christine?" Meg flew to sit next to her, placing her hand on her friend's shoulder. "What is it?"

"O–oh, I've been...foolishly trying to hide it...make this visit pleasant...Your big day is coming after all..."

"Not before yours..." Meg's eyes went to Christine's middle.

"I've ...been having pains all morning...I just...it wasn't enough to concern myself with...could've been anything. I've had false labor before..." her friend confessed. "But...now, I–I think...y–yes...my water just broke..."

"I'll let your driver know..." I stood up.

"N–no time..." The Vicomtesse shook her head, moaning through another contraction. "The..ride will be too bumpy...Safer here..." Knowing she was right, I instead hurried to the kitchen. Before I could open my mouth to let them know, Erik was standing in front of me, eyes tear-stained and full of exhausted defeat.

"I–I know..." He sighed, gently moving me out of the way as he approached the sofa with quiet determination. Antoinette was right behind him, her arms full of clean linens.

"Meg, keep an eye on the water I've started to boil. Sarah, I might need you to steady Erik...I'll do the same for Christine." I could only nod my agreement, moving to Erik's side as I placed a hand on his shoulder. It was clear that he was knowledgeable, having studied medical books along with other subjects and genres. Carrying that knowledge out, however, was an entirely different matter, especially with a patient as special to him as Christine. He hesitated before taking a seat on the coffee table in front of her trembling legs.

"I–I can't...Th–the Vicomte—"

"...will have nothing but gratitude for the hands that deliver our baby..." Christine spoke up against his doubt with stubborn confidence. "I believe in you, Erik..." Those words coaxed him to finally make eye contact with her as she smiled at him with a slight nod.

"I'll walk you both through everything," Antoinette assured them, perceiving that despite Christine's experience and Erik's knowledge, both would need her voice of guidance. "Erik, you just get ready to catch the baby and let us know if you see anything wrong."

"V–very well..." Erik gulped, his tear-streaked face quickly draining of color as he lowered himself to the table. I gently tightened my grip on his shoulder, spreading the linens out over his shaking hands.

"You can do this..." I whispered in his ear, and he turned slightly to face me.

"Will...you pray us through?"

"Of course..." I smiled, whispering one continuous prayer until the sound of Christine's son's first cry replaced his mother's screams, filling the cottage and summoning Meg from the kitchen to share in her friend's celebration. Even then, I lifted up more prayers of relieved gratitude. Once he'd cut the cord, Erik carefully placed the newborn infant into the Vicomtesse's arms before silently returning to the kitchen.

I gave him a few moments before joining him; he was doubled over the sink, fingers tightly gripping the counter edges as his body shook with emotion and waves of nausea. I knew no words would help or truly speak to everything he must have been going through. I couldn't even decipher which mood he might be in more than another. As he finally slid to the floor, I silently stepped past him, dampening a cloth before sitting down beside him to tenderly wipe his face. After a few moments, he reached up to take both the cloth and the hand holding it, pressing both to his eyes, then down his scarred cheek to his collarbone. "She—believed in me...J–just as you said she did...a–and...I still couldn't have done it....Not without His help..."

"Sometimes, the first baby step of faith is a giant one..." I offered a reassuring smile, even though he had yet to look my way.

Instead, he closed his eyes, taking deep breaths until they became soft and even. I knew the sort of sleep that was overtaking him quickly; where a moment of heightened anxiety and emotions would steal every ounce of energy and strength. There was no time for any further words. Instead, I went to borrow a pillow and blanket from Antoinette, seeing to his comfort as best as possible without making him move from the floor, and then I reluctantly left his side so that I could help our hosts with their newest guest.

The driver was finally informed, but rather than subject mother and child to the bumpy ride back home, he offered to fetch Raoul and the girls. Allowing Meg time to dote upon Christine and the baby, Antoinette and I simultaneously decided to do some cleaning before fixing supper. When she saw Erik fast asleep on the floor, she clicked her tongue with a shake of the head. "I'm surprised he made it all the way through that...It was far too much to ask of him..."

"If not for the Holy Spirit dwelling inside of him, he would have fled the moment he laid eyes on her this afternoon..."

"You had your hand in that too, dear...." She filled a large pot with water. "Even though I was his aide much of his life, I still had my limits...I could never have gotten as close to him as you have..."

"He still respects you, I've noticed." I counted out potatoes to peel.

"Oh, my dear..." She glanced at him, lowering her voice. "It is a mask. I know what he is capable of. I know he would never attack me, but...I still hide behind the same sternness I show to the girls that I teach. I suppose he's figured that out, but I feel it is better to be safe. As good as our intentions might be, we can never know how we'll truly act until the heat of the moment is upon us."

"That's true..." I nodded slightly, reminded of Erik's and my first meeting. "He has changed though. Perhaps now your friendship *could* grow deeper."

"Perhaps..." She nodded in partial agreement, though her tone was still thick with doubt.

Raoul and the girls arrived shortly before supper was ready to be served, and all focus throughout the meal was on Christine and the baby, who they named Gustave to honor her father's memory. Erik remained asleep despite the girls' excited chatter, and so the Vicomte actually seemed slightly disappointed to not see his former rival when he heard of his involvement. "I'd like to shake his hand...Are you sure you can't wake him?"

"He needs his rest..." Antoinette spoke up. "Perhaps in the morning, if you can stay, of course..."

"We won't put you out..."

"Nonsense! You and Christine will have my bed. I'll room with Meg and the girls...Sarah, will the sofa be comfortable for you, now that it's been cleaned?"

"Of course!" I smiled, and Antoinette nodded victoriously at Raoul.

"There it's settled. No one should feel the need to leave tonight."

"We are forever in your debt, Madame Giry." Raoul shook his head at her determination. "Anything we can give towards Meg's wedding or reception, please name it."

"I'll keep that in mind, but it really is not necessary."

"If you can insist, by all means, so can I...!" The Vicomte chuckled, and I silently hoped he would show Erik the same agreeable mood as he had now. Perhaps their interactions from now on would be pleasant instead of tense or awkward; surely by now the both of them could see that they each deserved some level of gratitude from the other.

    I did not get the chance to see the result of such hope the next morning, however. Sometime in the night, I was urgently shaken out of my slumber. "Sarah...we must go..." Although he was whispering, I could tell Erik's voice was still heavy with the previous day's emotions. Fumbling in the darkness, I found his hand and used it to help me sit up with an exhausted groan.

    "What's the rush...?" I yawned and stretched.

    "I just...I can't stay here..."

    "Oh, but Raoul was hoping to speak with you..."

    "That's precisely why we must go, now." He threw my comfortable blanket aside, pulling me to my feet. "I heard he was here but chose to not make an appearance...I did not wish to steal attention from their joy..." He guided me toward the door. "Nor will I allow my presence to shadow tomorrow morning."

    "Erik, you don't understand...He's not angry with you...He *wants* to talk with you...perhaps clear the air on everything..."

    "Even if that's true, Sarah, now is not the time..." He gently gripped my shoulders. "That baby needs their full attention. He's far too important...too fragile and helpless for me to take any of his parents' focus off of him. I won't have him neglected." At his vow of overwhelming concern for the newborn, I softened completely. I certainly should have thought of it before, what must have gone through his mind as he held that baby, even for the few seconds before he'd handed him over to his mother. Although I knew his presence in the morning wouldn't nearly affect the DeChagney couple quite as much as he was assuming, I also knew that he was still weak and very much emotional. With a sigh, I decided to change the subject as one final attempt at convincing him to stay.

"Are you sure you feel up to the journey?" At that, he gave my shoulders a slight squeeze.

"I managed to eat the portion of supper you set aside for me, and so far it hasn't given me any issues..." He paused for several moments, shuffling his feet. "I...apologize that...you saw me in that state..."

"There's no need..." I gently hugged him. "I'm glad you're feeling better, but as I said, I care about you. It will take a lot more than that to change my mind about helping you any way that I can..." He paused once more at that, slowly bringing his hand to my face. Another few moments passed, and it seemed as though he were debating within himself before he finally dropped his hand with a slight caress to my hairline.

"We'd best get going. You may finish your sleep on the way...." Knowing his mind was set, I shoved aside any potential argument, silently following him out to the carriage. Once we were settled, he draped his cloak over me like a blanket; I had nothing to do other than lean against him to steady myself as I allowed the rocking and creaking of the vehicle to lull me back to sleep.

****

The day before Meg's wedding, we traveled back into the country to ensure we were there on time. I would be staying in the Giry's house, and Erik opted to sleep in the loft above the stables. Meg was thrilled to see me again; in the time between visits I'd figured out that she'd grown up surrounded by other girls, and the past six years she'd been so secluded even from

Christine, save for the occasional visit; the most recent one being when Gustave was born. It was understandable that she befriended me so quickly, and for the same reason why Christine would have wanted that much-needed alone time with Meg to focus entirely on making up for lost time. Since we were sharing her room, Meg and I stayed up for hours, discussing and calming her nerves while I constantly dodged her questions about Erik and my feelings for him. To even think such things would surely end up in disappointment. He'd made his own feelings perfectly clear.

And so I steered the conversation back to her hopes and dreams. She and Robert of course wanted children, and hoped the Opera House would be repaired. Since her groom was a wood carver, she knew he'd volunteer to do the finishing touches, and then her children and the DeChagney children would begin the next generation of performers. By the time I finally fell asleep, I vowed to myself to ask Erik about beginning the repairs himself.

The next day came quickly—almost too quickly. As I got ready, I knew something was off. I refused to ruin Meg's day, however, and so I threw a smile on my face and helped her, Antoinette, and Christine's daughters get ready for the ceremony. When the Vicomtesse stopped in to drop the girls off and bid last minute wishes to Meg, she informed me that she and her husband had finally caught up with Erik in his attempt to seclude himself in the stables until the ceremony, when he planned on slipping into the back of the church. Robert had arrived shortly after the former rivals had made peace with each other, and Christine had led the girls away to give the men space to get to know each other a bit more. The girls needed to get ready anyway, and Gustave had begun to grow restless waiting for his mother to get settled again.

The chat between Raoul, Robert, and Erik, must have gone well; they'd somehow convinced Erik to play the church organ while I stood as a bridesmaid. I wondered silently if Antoinette had said something about Erik's talent the morning after Gustave's birth. However it had come about didn't matter, however. In watching him, I could tell he was having doubts about everything. Having his back to everyone helped though, and the moment his fingers brushed against the keys, he was immediately swept away into his element.

About halfway through the reception, I felt myself weakening. It had to have been caused by a lack of sleep the night before, I reasoned silently. Even so, I lowered myself to a chair while mostly everyone else danced, closing my eyes for what I thought was just a moment. When I opened them, however, I was back in Meg's room, the last colors of sunset peering through the window. I could hear Erik and Antoinette out in the hallway. Had it not been for their stubborn tones, I would have gone out to them. "Oh, I can see it perfectly clearly, Erik! She was not used to the darkness of your caverns to begin with, and now she's not used to the sun and fresh air. The extremes have made her ill...."

"What do you want me to do?" Erik's flustered voice hissed. "What can you honestly picture me doing?"

"Oh, you're ready for honesty, hmm? Well, since you are not married, she should not be living in such seclusion with you. Until you're ready for that, you should take her back home to be with her family. She needs them right now."

"I'm the closest she has to family now, Antoinette." Erik spoke quietly after a long pause. "I'm all she has in the world."

"Oh, I...I see..." I could picture Antoinette's twisted face as she thought everything over. "No, you're not. She has me. She'll stay here."

"That's your solution? Separation by at least half a day's journey?" I could hear the panic in his voice, and it was all I could do to not burst right through the door and squeeze his hand.

"You...don't *have* to stay in the city, Erik. There's plenty of land out here...You can start again..." A heavy silence fell between the two, and it wasn't long before sleep carried me away once again.

****

The next morning, I woke up to find Erik sitting by my bed, my hand between both of his. Though his eyes were on me, he was so lost in his thoughts that it didn't register that I was awake until I attempted to sit up. "No...you need your rest..." He quietly stopped me.

"Erik, I..."

"No...let me speak." He rubbed his face, wiping at dried-on tears in the process. "I did this...I made you sick..."

"You did nothing of the sort, Erik. I made my choice. We've both agreed that I was never your prisoner..." I gently took his hand again.

"True as that may be, Sarah, I...I need to leave you here for a while. I spoke with Antoinette, and...you need to stay here with her...You need each other."

"What will you do?" I felt my eyes well up, knowing that he was right but worried about him just the same. He brought his hand to my face, caressing while subtly brushing my tears away with his thumb.

"I won't be far. I'll come visit often..But I must figure out my life now."

"I...was thinking about the Opera House, Erik...The repairs need to be started sometime by someone..."

"That's a possibility..." He slowly nodded. "But you just concentrate on getting better so that you can help Antoinette...Keep her company...She already misses her daughter terribly."

"And I already miss you..." I blurted with a sob. He gently pulled me into a hug, and I could tell he was fighting back his own tears. "E–Erik...I..."

"Don't...please, don't say it...It will only hurt more..." He pulled back then, resting his hands on my shoulders. We searched each other's eyes for several moments, and I hoped he could see in mine what he would not allow me to say. "Now then...I'll let Antoinette know you're awake and that you'll be wanting a pastry with your breakfast." He let a small smile appear across his face as he stood up. "It's best that I leave now. I've a long journey ahead..."

"Take care of yourself?" I clung to his hand just a bit longer.

"I will...I promise..." This time, he met my gaze, and I knew he would be true to his word. I managed a tiny nod, and as he left, I fell back on the pillow and wept. *I love you...*

****

****SIX****

I stayed in bed for at least another week. It wasn't just from sickness or missing Erik. I was also afraid I'd let something slip. And so, whenever Antoinette brought me food or checked in on me, I pretended to be asleep. Of course I felt bad for doing so; she and I were in the same boat. But I simply could not bring myself to be sociable.

When I was finally feeling well enough, I allowed her to convince me to sit outside. I had to admit that the fresh air felt good, but it did nothing to ease the heartache.

One particularly beautiful afternoon, she brought the tea outside. As usual, she offered me a cup and a pastry. As usual, I politely declined both. Rather than giving me a sympathetic shoulder squeeze before returning inside with a sigh like she always did, however, she sat down in the chair next to mine. "It's not that I don't understand, my dear. Your feelings are perfectly clear and normal. Do not think that a day goes by where I don't miss my husband." I finally met her gaze then; I'd completely forgotten that she wasn't just lonely for her daughter. "At least you know Erik is still alive..." She offered me a tight smile.

"I–I'm sorry...I didn't...I mean...I *knew* of course, but..."

"Thank you, dear...He was a good man...and wherever he is, I know he's proud of the woman Meg grew up to be. At the same time, he would not like for me to waste my tears on him. I know he's happy, and he wants me to be as well."

"It can't be helped, though...Grief takes a lifetime..."

"Oh, I know, dear, I know. But my point is, seeing the way you and Erik are...He wouldn't want you to just sit here watching the road day after day for him to return. Leaving you was hard enough for him. If he knew how you were taking it, he'd be right back here getting nothing done for his future..and for yours..."

"He...doesn't think of me like that..." I looked down at my hands.

"Oh, I think he does, my dear. He was the first to notice that you had collapsed at the reception, and never left your side except for when the doctor was examining you. Even then, he lingered just outside your door. He cares so much more for you than he wants to admit, even to himself. It's just that Christine's rejection made him very wary of acting so impulsively again."

"I...never thought of that... I guess I was so selfishly focused on my own pain..." I teared up yet again. It made perfect sense. How could I have been so blind? She slowly pulled me into a comforting hug.

"It's quite alright, dear...we're only human after all..." She again offered me the tea and pastry, and this time, I didn't say no.

****

A week later, I was sweeping out the front room when there was a knock on the door. As I set the broom aside, I heard the unmistakable sound of a baby crying. Assuming it was Christine, I grinned, opened the door, and was met by Erik thrusting an infant into my arms. "M—make it stop..." His face and voice were thick with exhaustion; I didn't even get a chance to start telling him how happy I was to see him again before he plopped face down onto the sofa.

A million questions swirled in my mind as I held the baby, but those would have to wait. A quick touch told me exactly what the problem was. The moment I pulled off the diaper, Erik flew off the couch with the loudest, sickened groan, glaring in my direction while hiding the bottom half of his face with one of the throw pillows. "Well? How do you think *she* feels?" I suppressed a giggle. We had no clean diapers, of course, and so I cut a piece out of an extra set of sheets that Antoinette was going to use for rags anyway. As I busied myself with cleaning the baby up and finding something to feed to her, I glanced over at Erik, who by now had returned to the couch and was watching me quietly. "Who is she, anyway?" I brought her over and sat down next to him.

"I...I don't know..." He shook his head. "I found her a couple days ago in the Opera House stables...There was a note...her mother couldn't take care of her. I...gave her some milk from the market, but...I didn't know what else to do...I...just know that she's not going to the gypsies or any orphanage. I won't let her."

"Of course not. No child deserves to go through what you did...yourself included." I rested my hand on his arm. "I'm glad you brought her here. I missed you..."

"And I you..." He lowered his gaze.

"Have...you decided anything yet?"

"No...My future's still one blank page...I'm sorry to disappoint you..."

"Erik, no...Any disappointment on my part would be my own doing. I shouldn't put so much pressure or expectation on your shoulders. You're not responsible for my happiness." I offered him a reassuring smile.

"Then...you're content to stay here? Watch little Janelle until I can secure her future?"

"That's a lovely name, Erik...And yes, I'll be happy to look after her for you."

"Good...Thank you, Sarah...I owe you much more than I can give..." He stood up.

"You're leaving already?"

"It's for the best..." He nodded, squeezing my shoulder. "I'll be back plenty of times to check on the both of you. Give my regards to Antoinette..." With that, he was gone as quickly as he'd come. Left alone, I dropped my gaze to the now sleeping infant. She couldn't have been more than maybe one or two months old, and already she had quite the head of light brown hair. I wondered about her parents, specifically her mother. What circumstances would have forced her to do such a thing? To have held and fed and certainly loved this child for over a month, only to leave her for a stranger to find...whatever the reason, it must have been urgent. Lifting up a silent prayer for someone I'd probably never meet, I gently wrapped her blanket tighter around her before drifting off to sleep myself.

****

It took Antoinette several hours to finish fuming at the absent Erik. Hours that I spent finding a makeshift cradle for Janelle in my room. Of course I took my own sweet time; no amount of movie viewings or imaginings could have aptly prepared me for the sheer volume of the ballet instructor's wrath, and *she* was one of Erik's closest friends! Perhaps that was why she was so upset; once again Erik had disappointed her and plopped another surprise in her lap. To be sure, I tried to explain that *I* would take full care of Janelle, but my voice fell on deaf ears.

By the time she calmed down, supper had grown cold. I didn't dare mention it though. Thankfully, Janelle was a sound sleeper; the last thing Antoinette needed was a reminder. I instead tried to get a conversation going about the beautiful day and how we should invite the DeChagneys over for a picnic soon, following Meg and Robert's return from their honeymoon. That brought a smile to Antoinette's face finally; it was almost as if she had forgotten her daughter was set to return at the beginning of the following week. We were soon planning out the whole menu, and pleasant laughter filled the cottage once again.

****

    An invitation was also sent to Erik, and from the look on his face upon his arrival, he hadn't even thought about what Antoinette's reaction to Janelle would have been. Instead, he immediately scooped the baby girl up in his arms before taking notice of the other guests. This action on his part caused everyone else to stare, wide-eyed and puzzled. Christine's daughters in particular looked up from their little brother, and Lottie exclaimed almost too loudly, "Oh, look, Mama! Monsieur Erik and Mademoiselle Sarah had a baby too!" That did it. Erik finally looked up at the old familiar sound of laughter, his face reddening. I quickly touched his arm.
    "They don't know, Erik...They're only little girls..." Even then, he didn't begin to calm down until his eyes fell on the stern face of Madame Giry.
    "Well, what did you expect, Erik? Of course they're curious." We could all tell she wanted to say more, but the feast before us took priority. Gradually, Erik and I explained Janelle's origins as best as we could, finishing with Erik's intentions of raising the child as his own. Satisfied, Meg and Christine took over the conversation, catching up and exchanging hopes for the future. The girls grew restless and started a game of tag, and the husbands slowly made their way to the carriages to discuss

current events. It was then that Antoinette recruited Erik and I to bring some things inside before taking the dessert out to our guests. Only then did Erik reluctantly hand Janelle over to me; she needed changing again, anyway. Once I was in my room, I heard their hushed voices start what I just knew would turn into an argument. "Well?" Antoinette spoke first, of course.

"Well, what?"

"What are your plans, Erik? Sarah is not going to be your nanny forever."

"I'm working on it, woman!" I heard the clattering of dishes being thrust into the sink. "Just what you told me to do!"

"Working on what? That tells me nothing!"

"If you must know, I've purchased some land and I'm building a house. You're fortunate that your invitation reached me while I was getting some things from the cellars."

"And what of Sarah?"

"You said yourself that you won't allow her to leave with me..." His voice was cold and low.

"That's not all I said, and you know it! When your house is built, Janelle will need a woman to help raise her, and Sarah already loves her. Even a marriage of convenience–"

"No."

"Erik, I–"

"I said, no."

"Erik for goodness sake! You cannot deny the fact that you care for her even a little bit. And you know that one does not throw water on a spark if you want a fire to grow. You tend to that spark and feed it."

"I'll only hurt her, Antoinette. Don't ask me to feed her expectations when we both know–"

"That she's not Christine? Of course she's not. But she's not me, either. I will not allow Janelle to stay here if you're only going to treat Sarah as the occasional helper at your every whim's beck and call!"

"Are you done?" His voice grew shaky. I couldn't tell if he was on the verge of tears or an angry outburst, and I wasn't about to show my face to find out which.

"Not quite. Just think about it, won't you? Think about Sarah...her feelings...her reputation if more people see her with a baby and no wedding ring...You heard all the rumors about yourself from people who knew nothing of the truth. Imagine what that will eventually do to her."

"I need some fresh air. If I don't return, tell Sarah...Just...think of something." Seconds later, the door closed. Minutes afterwards, I slowly made my appearance. Antoinette threw me a sympathetic smile, and I could tell that she knew I had heard every word.

****

It was months before I saw Erik again. Not a letter was sent; only the occasional few bills to help with Janelle's care. I filled my days helping Antoinette prepare for the coming winter. Sometimes, we'd visit Christine or Meg. Mostly, we watched Janelle grow from drinking only milk to eating creamed vegetables. Teething was difficult, of course, but Antoinette knew just what to do.

Then, around the time when my family would be preparing for Thanksgiving, he arrived. He didn't speak a word, only took my hand and brought me out to the back garden. I shivered in the cold, but not for long. With a shaky hand, he held out a ring...*The* ring. "Before you give your answer, Sarah...I don't want you to get any ideas. Antoinette...suggested a marriage of convenience, and that's what this will be. You'll have a room of your own...You'll be aptly provided for, and your reputation won't be ruined. I can give you everything, Sarah, but not my heart. You must understand that."

I was silent for the longest time, my eyes brimming with tears. My first thought was, *What's the point, then?* But I thought about Janelle, and I knew what Antoinette had said was true. I had grown to love her as my own, and I knew she needed us both. I had to do this for her. Still unable to speak, I simply nodded. He quietly slid the ring onto my finger before making his way inside. I slowly followed to find him already holding Janelle. Silently, I prayed that God would guard my heart, mind, words, and actions, and that He'd give me the strength for the future ahead.

****

The wedding was small, with only Antoinette, Meg, and Robert present. It came quickly, within two weeks of the proposal. When it was time for the kiss, Erik simply brushed his lips against my forehead before immediately boarding his carriage. It was already packed, and as soon as Antoinette handed Janelle up to me, we took off. No cake, no celebration.

The house he'd built was beautiful but small and cozy–a single story with a sitting room, eat-in kitchen, and separate work shed for his music and art. There was of course an outhouse, but Erik said he planned on building a connecting passageway in the spring for the cold or rainy days.

For the time being, he showed me to my room which was down the hall from his, with Janelle's nursery in between. He then went to unload the carriage, leaving me to explore my quarters on my own. The room was furnished simply and practically, but I couldn't help but notice a few personalized touches. He'd taken the curtains I'd purchased for the lair and hung them in the windows along with little mobiles of the shattered mirror glass; the setting sunlight reflecting off of them and dancing all over the walls. He'd also brought over my chosen books and built a little bookcase for them next to an armchair upholstered in a soft fabric of royal blue. The quilt upon the bed was of a blue rose print on a white background, and he had even gone so far as to carve a large rose into the headboard. Across the room was a large wardrobe containing my dresses from the lair, and a stand with a wash basin and pitcher of teal porcelain completed the furnishings.

When he finished unloading the carriage, he returned to stand in the doorway. "Do...you see anything else you might want or need that I've forgotten..?"

"No...this is really more than enough, Erik. Thank you..." I smiled softly, but he didn't return it.

"Good night then..." he slowly left, closing the door behind him. *So it begins...* I thought with a sigh before readying myself for bed. I refused to cry. He couldn't help what he felt, and it would be wrong for me to try to guilt or force him into feeling anything else.

****

****SEVEN****

The winter months passed slowly, but in a blur. It was like being in the lair all over again, when he was still angry. This time, however, there was Janelle to keep us occupied. We quickly fell into a routine, silently agreeing to alternate who got up to check on her whenever she woke up crying. As spring approached, however, Erik spent more and more time in his work shed long into the night. Several times, when it should have been his turn, I'd wake up anyway to find the candles in his window still burning. I didn't complain though. Even if I wanted to, he always made himself scarce unless his hunger brought him to the kitchen table. I could feel anger and resentment building up inside me, but that only made me more bitter. I hated how selfish I was being. I of all people should know and understand better. Besides, it wasn't as if he hadn't made himself perfectly clear. This was my choice, and I had agreed not for my desires to be fulfilled, but for Janelle's sake alone. If there was one thing that we absolutely agreed upon to the point where it could have easily been the center of our marriage, it was that Janelle would grow up without a single doubt that she was loved.

And so I tried to rest in that thought. Besides, this was all very new to Erik, having a wife and child and house of his own. It would all take quite a bit of getting used to.

One rainy morning in early April, I went about the usual breakfast preparations and getting Janelle ready for the day. It wasn't until I was putting the food on the table when I glanced outside. The candle was still lit in Erik's workshed window. Never before had he spent the entire night; there was no fireplace, so while Erik was adaptable and the building was well insulated, the chill usually eventually persuaded him back to the house.

Still, I had to set my concern aside until Janelle was fed and put in her bassinet. Handing her the rattling toy Erik had crafted for her, I grabbed my shawl and ran over, ignoring the mud puddles soaking through my slippers. Thankfully, the door was unlocked, and when I finally laid my eyes on him, my heart fell. He was slumped over his desk, his face covered in a feverish sweat. "Erik?" I bit my lip. "Erik, you're sick...Can you try to walk?"

"No...need...to finish..." He mumbled, shakily reaching for his pen and ink in the completely opposite direction from their actual placement.

"Later...Let's get you inside..." I gently tugged on his arm. Thankfully, he slowly rose to his feet and let me lead him across the yard, through the house, and into his room. The moment his head hit the pillow, though, he passed out once again.

For three days, he slept. For three days, I was completely on my own to care for both of them and the house. When I wasn't crying, I was praying; it was all I really knew to do. There was no way I knew of to get in touch with a doctor or even Antoinette, and to leave Erik was out of the question.

On the fourth day, I was holding Janelle on my lap while replacing the cold cloth on his forehead. I may have been crying–I'd grown just about numb to the sensation of tears rolling down my face over trails of dried ones. As much as I believed and trusted in God and His promises, the nagging, fearful thought kept returning to my mind...What if? What if he never gets better? It scared and frustrated me how much I'd grown to depend on him, but here in his world...our world now...that was just the way things were. I could, of course, return to Antoinette, but sooner or later she'd notice my inability to age.

I lowered my gaze to Erik once again, trying to shake off my selfish fears. His bare chest rose and fell in soft, even breaths. He'd look so peaceful were it not for his furrowed brow. I brought my hand down from the cloth to caress his scars. As far into his nightmare as he was, the wrinkles between his eyes disappeared. *Oh, Erik....if only you would allow me to show you just how much I–* "Papa..." Janelle's first word rang out through the silence, crystal clear. Amazingly, Erik stirred beneath my hand.

"Janelle...I'm here my darling..." he mumbled before slowly opening his eyes. It took him several moments to get his bearings. "Y–she spoke...?" He looked up at me.

"Y–yes..just now..." I was sobbing again, this time from relief. There was so much I wanted to do, but I stopped myself at simply squeezing his hand. "You were asleep for three days...I–I thought...Oh, never mind. You're better now...That's what matters..."

"I...didn't mean to frighten you..."

"No...it's quite alright..." I smiled softly. "You needed the rest...Are you hungry?" At that, he nodded.

"Leave Janelle with me?" He forced himself into a sitting position before I could protest. Silently, I handed her over before going to heat up the previous night's stew.

Over the next couple days, Erik gradually regained his strength. Still, I insisted he stay put a little bit longer, just to be safe. He didn't protest all that much; I figured he felt too guilty about worrying me to be stubborn. At any rate, it was nice seeing him around the house more often.

One night, after putting Janelle to bed, I went into his room to gather his dishes and bid him goodnight. His eyes were closed, and so I pulled the blanket up before picking up his tray. Just then, I felt his hand on my arm. "Leave the dishes for the morning…I want to talk to you."

"Alright…" I went to pull the chair over.

"No…come sit with me. We are married after all…" he moved over on the bed. Suddenly overcome by shyness, I slowly obeyed, letting him take my hands once I had settled next to him against the headboard. For a moment, he closed his eyes again, and I began to think he was fighting back sleep. Ever so slightly, however, I noticed his lips moving in what I could only assume to be a whispered prayer. He then took a deep breath before opening his eyes again; they were filled with a combination of emotions I couldn't quite put my finger on. Variations of fear and deep sadness mixed with the faintest glimmer of hope. Whatever words he was about to say, I knew then that my response could serve to either feed that hope or smother the flame completely. If he weren't holding my hands, I would have thrown my arms around him then in a comforting embrace. I almost told him he needn't say anything if he only wished to be held, but I could tell that if he didn't speak now, as important as it might be, the opportunity would be lost entirely with the moment as it passed us by. Even to rest my head against his shoulder would risk him putting off whatever was burdening his mind until another time that may not come, giving him the idea that I was too sleepy to listen.

And so I simply sat with him for several minutes in what felt like a sort of testing of my patience, friendship, and loyalty… to see just how long I could bear to be his silent rock while waves of turmoil crashed inside of him. Finally, just as sleepiness was indeed creeping upon my eyelids, he took one more deep breath before speaking. "Do you remember when I had to leave you in your sickness with Antoinette?"

"Vividly..." I nodded, struggling against the emotions that accompanied the memory.

"Well I never told you this...but had Antoinette not come up with the idea herself, I still probably would have gone. I could not let you or anyone bear witness to what followed. What you saw after Gustave's birth wasn't even the half of it. It was a part of me I had only feared to have existed...a part of myself that should have only appeared in nightmares or wild imaginings...You brought me to the place where I needed to be, but this was an all-out battle which I had to fight alone, with just God and I facing my greatest enemy.

"You see, Sarah, I spent my entire life relying on the darkness for security and survival. It served to be my closest companion...When that same darkness made you sick, it...shook me to my very core...To think that my safety could prove harmful to you...I just knew I had to be apart from you. And so all that time, I was agonizing over that realization...allowing God to banish that darkness from my life...from my innermost being...ripping it out like a deeply rooted weed instead of the friend and ally I thought it so sincerely to be.

"Part of me questioned why I cared so much to go through all that just so I wouldn't have to stay away from you...My answer then was to remind myself of your friendship...How I couldn't remain angry with you at your disobedience...How you were the one to make me realize that letting go of things we tend to cling to allows us to receive the far better ones God has in store. I...should have seen it then, what I see now, but...I was stubborn...focused more on the blank white page of my future now that the darkness was gone and the counter-attacks diminished from waking nightmares to lingering doubt and uncertainty. All I saw myself as was a pile of shattered mirror glass in the blinding sunlight...too broken to be fixed, too jumbled and dirty to be of any use. I..was so lost...so scared...Finding Janelle, though, it..was like finding the first stepping stone across a raging river. I finally had a purpose...but even though she took all my energy and attention, you never left my mind. At first, I thought it to be God's way of pointing out the help with Janelle I needed... Perhaps it was partly that. And so with that thought in mind, built this house and furnished your room in the hopes of some sort of living arrangement being worked out. I knew I'd have to do a lot of convincing where Antoinette was concerned, but I chose to postpone the thought until after the work was complete.

"It was in my final trip to the caverns that I spotted that pile of neglected mirror glass. I never gave it a thought; I just... automatically began crafting it into what is now hanging in your window. It was as if I were simply a pair of hands, not knowing what the final product would look like but working towards it anyway. When I did finally see that it was finished, I saw it as a reflection of how I was feeling...Just broken pieces dangling by threads. I was angry...feeling like God created it through me only to remind me of what I'd never forgotten. Still, I couldn't toss it aside. He meant for it to be made, and so I figured at least you would get some enjoyment from it.

"Then, when the idea and execution of the wedding came, I felt like I was back to being that pile of brokenness all over again. It was too soon...Your room may have been ready, but I certainly wasn't, and having you fully present to help with Janelle allowed me time to agonize once again.

"That's why I've been hiding myself, Sarah...I was scared...scared of you, scared of marriage...scared of not knowing what to do with the future to provide for Janelle...for you...Once again I wondered why I cared so much about you and your thoughts of me. Only this time when I tried to satisfy myself with reminders of your friendship, I was left still feeling empty. It was in watching you with Janelle that the truth finally dawned on me. It was so easy for me to recognize and accept the fact that you love her as your own daughter, and so...why was it so difficult a concept that you loved me as well? It was so simple...so obvious...And...I finally realized...I realized what your motivation has been all this time. You've proven to me countless times that you're different...You truly care for me...Want to be with me to the point of sacrificing your own happiness. At first, I thought you to be as foolish as I was with Christine, only I didn't want to cause you the pain that she did me. But in trying to avoid hurting you, I was hurting you anyway...A stolen ring...a borrowed gown from Meg's own wedding...no family or celebration...a wedding night alone...a husband barely there to live up to his vows and promises to share in raising Janelle...none of it was what you dreamed of or even expected when I asked you. All I did was give you more and more reason to be miserable...to change your mind and resent me instead.

"And so...moments ago, I was praying for the right words...to either somehow free you from this arrangement, or...to win your heart again..." Releasing my hands, he closed his eyes as silent tears fell. My heart sank as he turned his head away; he was bracing for rejection.

"Oh, Erik..." I whispered around the lump forming in my throat. At the sound of my voice, he sniffled, his lips parting in preparation for the impending sobs as he covered his face. *Oh no you don't...not if I can help it...* Gently moving his hand away from his cheek, I replaced it with soft trails of kisses along each line, bump, and scar. "You don't have to win my heart...it was always yours...and it always will be..." Ever so gradually, he turned his head to meet my lips with his own. Although it was entirely his idea to do so, he paused the moment our lips touched. With each inhale and exhale, only the continuous flow of tears and the trembling of his lower lip served to remind me that time had not in fact completely frozen. It was as if he had to break through a barrier of memories from Christine's kiss, and so I forced myself to hold back on my lips' response; as much as I wanted to show him I returned his feelings, I knew he needed my patience now more than ever.

My theory was proven correct when he pulled back, studying my face, searching for the slightest trace of a mask that might be covering my fear or disgust. I blinked back tears as I recalled watching his face after his first kiss...How that glimmer of hope so quickly turned into tears of crippling heartbreak. He brought his hand to my face then, caressing my hairline as a smile gingerly appeared before me.

"You...truly love me...?" The tone of his voice threatened to shatter me inside. I wrapped my arms around him to steady us both, snuggling against him.

"I absolutely do, Erik...I love you so much..." I nestled my head against his shoulder before looking up at him. Now, it was my turn to throw out my own last thread of hope...to brace myself for his honest answer and brave whatever outcome it would bring. "Are you sure, though, that this is what *you* want? That you wouldn't be merely settling?" At this, he laughed openly yet tearfully, as if a dam had burst from in front of his every emotion.

"Oh, Sarah...I've wanted this all my life...to be loved...truly loved....for who I am, outside and inside...past, present, future...*I was foolish to chase after an incomplete love for so long...I was the fool...not you...*You saw what I couldn't...what I *wouldn't* allow myself to see or feel...But now that I have seen your love for me, and that you were living out the definition of true love all this time, I know that I've felt that same way towards you for quite a while now. I was just so caught up in my own idea of love that I completely missed it. Now I realize that with Christine, I would have been settling. With you...my every dream...my deepest desire...I'd be freeing us both...Freeing our hearts...I love you..." He gently lifted my chin to close the distance between our lips once again, sliding his fingers around to caress the side of my neck. This time, I followed his lead, matching his readiness in my response and allowing more of my bottled-up emotions to flow through.

By the time we pulled apart several moments later, his tender, fervent caresses had loosened my hair so that it fell like a curtain around us both as he sank into my arms, weeping and breathless. Letting my own tears fall, I traced little circles on his back, soothing him and silently allowing him to feel. Having studied his story for so long and now knowing him as I did, I could easily guess what must have been surging through his mind and heart. Relief seemed to be so insufficient a word for it, and yet it was the first I could identify as to what we were both sharing in that moment. Pure, sweet, overwhelming relief...to know we loved and were loved in return by each other...it was indeed a dream...a prayer fulfilled. My one hand still stroking his back, I brought my other one down to brush at his tears. "It's alright..." I whispered, letting a smile dry my own eyes. "I'm here...You never have to spend another night alone...Never..." At this, he finally found his voice. Raising himself into a more steady sitting position, he gently grasped my hand on his face and lowered it.

"No, Sarah...I...I can't let you stay...I don't trust myself. If we continue this, I...I won't be able to control...I'll hurt you...take you..." At the candid innocence in his voice, I felt my heart shatter all over again for him, and I leaned my forehead against his chest just long enough to swallow the lump forming in my throat. When I once more met his gaze, the doubt in his eyes only strengthened my determination to show him how I truly felt about him.

"You wouldn't be taking me forcibly, my love...We'd be giving each other ourselves freely...Out of the love we share..." I brought his hand closer so I could rest my cheek against his palm. "We are married after all..." Using his own words as a reminder, I finally succeeded in causing his smile to return, pushing through all his anxieties.

"As long as you're sure..." Seeing his eyes still searching for a mask, I kissed him again, guiding his hand to my side with a gentle, reassuring squeeze.

"I've never been more sure of anything, save my faith in God..." I smiled up at him. "I love you, Erik...I trust you...Of that I am certain..."

"And I you, Sarah..." Blinking back another wave of tears, he pulled me into a tighter embrace, pressing his trembling lips against mine. "And I you..."

****

The next day, I moved into his...*our* room. I was now his wife in every sense of the word. The thought of growing old could never have made me any happier. My room would become a temporary guest room, although I had a feeling our family would eventually grow.

Erik soon busied himself with expanding the workshed so I could have space to write and do my crafts. The outhouse got its connection to the main house as promised, via a tunnel underground that ended in stairs far enough away that there was no threat of leaks or stench, and the outhouse itself was expanded so that the short walk from the stairs to the privy was sheltered. This allowed for the rare convenience of a separate wash room with both a tub and shower. Erik had done his research well when he was in my world.

This tunnel also provided a way for us to work on hobbies when the shed was inaccessible due to weather. What started as a small country cottage was turning into the equivalent of a two-story house with more than enough room for everyone, especially with how quickly Janelle was growing.

Whoever her parents were, we couldn't help but notice her early love for music. Almost as soon as she was talking, she was singing along to the lullabies we sang to her each night or if she needed comfort. Then, by the time she turned two, she was making up her own songs, wandering around the house as if it were one big stage. "I think you've got yourself a pupil!" I giggled to Erik one afternoon as he was telling me of her antics that morning while he'd allowed me to sleep in.

"I do believe you're right...And she won't be my only one for long..." He smiled, kissing my three-month baby bump.

"I always knew you'd be a wonderful father...You know what *you* missed out on, and so you give that to Janelle and soon this one..." I caressed his face.

"Well it's easy when I have you by my side..." He tenderly kissed each of my fingers.

"Did I mention how much I love you?"

"Not since lunchtime..." He chuckled.

"Really? Forgive me...that was so neglectful of me!" I giggled, moving my fingers through his hair.

"Well then we're both guilty, because I'm only just now telling you that I love you too..." He sat back up on the sofa next to me, and our lips met.

"I've got dishes to do...laundry to hang...Janelle's nap will be over soon..."

"You worry too much." My husband pulled me closer. "Let me spoil you for once."

"Erik, I'm fine..!" I giggled. "You're the one worrying too much!"

"I'm not worrying. I'm insisting. I want to take care of you...for your sake and the baby's..." He kissed my forehead, squeezing my hand gently.

"Well, I suppose I *could* get some sewing done..." I slightly rolled my eyes.

"Very good. You're learning." He chuckled.

"Yes, there's no use arguing with the Phantom of the—"

"Resort..." He growled, kissing me again to prevent further debate. Several minutes later, he left me to my sewing. I didn't get a whole lot of it done, however, because I was instead watching him and wondering how I could have possibly been this fortunate.

****

****EIGHT****

In the years that passed and as our children grew, the Opera House was gradually restored to its previous magnificence. It wasn't long before Janelle was at the right age to enter the dormitories under Meg's direction. Antoinette was semi-retired, but she offered her services as dorm mother. Janelle had inherited quite the unique, almost diva-like personality that, even with little Antoin and Claire running around the house, it still seemed so quiet and empty without their adopted sister bossing them around.

This is not to say we were apart for long; she was home for every holiday, and we made it a point to be at every performance, filling up the much-talked-about Box Five.

In training his own children, Erik had developed far more patience and tolerance if a performer failed to live up to his standards. Aside from the occasional wince, he sat through each performance with a smile on his face, rather than looking for a way to disrupt. "It helps that Carlotta has finally moved on..." he shrugged it off when I mentioned it. But I knew he was proud, as he should be. Already Antoin was displaying interest and talent in artwork and the piano, while little Claire, just four years old, had already plucked out a few notes on the harp. Mostly, though, she'd copy me with the housework and even take care of her doll like a wonderful mother. Once or twice, I caught her singing to 'Jeanine' when she should have been sleeping. Reluctant to discourage her, I let it slide.

One day, we arrived in Paris in time to watch the final rehearsal. While Erik took Antoin and Claire to visit the horses in the stables, I stood with Meg and Antoinette, watching the dancers. "It's uncanny..." Meg observed almost to herself.

"What is, dear?" Antoinette looked at her.

"Just...look at Janelle and tell me who she reminds you of..." We both followed her gaze in time to see Janelle stomp her foot.

"I can't *work* like this! You almost stepped on my toe! *Auntie Meg!!!*"

"Oh...my..." Antoinette's eyes grew.

"See? She'd just like..."

"Carlotta..." The older woman slowly nodded.

"Well, you can be sure Erik and I didn't teach her *that*!" I exclaimed. "I'll talk to her..." Pushing the observance to the back of my mind for the time being, I quickly went over and pulled Janelle aside.

"It's just not fair! I'm a singer, not a dancer! She *knows* that!" she sniffled.

"Now, Janelle, you know that Auntie Meg wants you to get experience in *all* the different groups. It will make you a better leading lady when the time comes."

"How?"

"You remember us telling you about how Auntie Christine stepped in as lead when she was needed? The audience notices that, Janelle. It shows how talented you really are."

"You...really think so?" She finally looked up at me with such big, tear-filled eyes that my first response could only have been to pull her close.

"I *know* so. Just remember, Auntie Meg has been through everything you're going through. Trust her. She knows what she's doing."

"O–okay, Mama..." She wiped her tears away, standing up.

"And, Janelle..."

"Yes, Mama?"

"An opera needs every single person in it to run properly. No role is more or less important than any other. The dancers and the singers aren't meant to compete with each other, but to complete each other."

"A–alright...I'll try to remember..." With a slow but genuine nod, she went back to join the others.

"I could not have said it better myself..." Antoinette came up behind me, smiling.

"If...if she is somehow Carlotta's...I don't want her to make the same mistakes." I sighed.

"Has Erik noticed?"

"Not yet...Believe me, it would show in his face even if he didn't voice it."

"Well, when he does, prepare for a storm..."

"Oh, I know..." I giggled nervously. "I know..."

****

The following spring, word spread of Carlotta's upcoming return to Paris. Naturally, it was the talk of the Opera House. Thankfully, Erik was preoccupied in the stables or shops with the younger ones whenever the subject came up. I knew that it would only be a matter of time before he found out, however, and so I figured it would be best to trigger the avalanche myself before it happened unexpectedly and caused more damage.

One late afternoon, he came in from taking care of the horses just as I was pulling a batch of brownies out of the oven. Replacing it with that night's casserole, I set it down on the counter next to the cookies and first batch of brownies. "*Someone's* been busy..." He grabbed a cookie and took a big bite before embracing and kissing me.

"Not that you're complaining, of course..." I pointed. Chuckling, he took a second cookie before looking around at everything.

"Let's see...no birthdays or holidays...still too early for any picnics..." .... "What's wrong...?" His smile faded into a suspicious expression.

"What on earth makes you think that?" I pouted.

"Just tell me..." He rolled his eyes, gently putting his hands on my shoulders.

"You...might want to sit down..." I bit my lip. Thankfully, the children were in their rooms, practicing their chosen hobbies. Soon after moving to the sofa, I told him of Carlotta's imminent visit that would surely include a trip to the Opera House for at least one performance.

"...I see..." Crumbs from the rest of the cookie fell from his clenched fist.

"....There's more...." I glanced down. Moments later, one entire pan of brownies had disappeared in the blur that was 'Hurricane Erik'. He left a trail of echoes of slamming doors through the downstairs tunnel before the walls shook in his final roar. Blinking, I calmly walked over to the basement door and opened it, calling, "It's only a possibility!"

"You had better hope it's just that!" He reappeared at the top of the stairs in no time.

"...Or what?" I met his glare evenly. "Erik, you can't just stop loving her because of who her mother *might* be. She's not her!"

"...I'm not in the mood for you to be right." he pouted, pushing past me.

"Erik..." I sighed, wrapping my arms around him from behind. "Whether she is or not, I think it's time to tell her the truth. If she is and Carlotta realizes and tells her before we can...imagine the confusion and hurt. She may never trust us again."

"Alright...alright...Dry your tears with a brownie..." He let out an exasperated sigh, stuffing the last of that batch into my mouth. "We'll get to Paris early. Take her on an outing. We'll tell her."

True to our word, we arrived in Paris the day before the next opening night. Meg and Antoinette did not need much convincing; in fact, they offered to give Antoin and Claire a day's worth of free introductory lessons to give Erik and I some alone time with Janelle. Although she was initially confused, she could not say no to the impromptu shopping spree and lunch at the cafe nearby. Afterwards, we walked her down to the river to watch the ducks from the bridge. "What's going on, Mama? Papa?" She finally looked up at us in such a way that we were reminded that she was now ten years old, no longer a completely naive little girl. Rather than answering directly, Erik kept his eyes on the feathered families swimming around us.

"Janelle, you see those ducklings? Remember what we told you about how families become families?"

"Of course...The mama and the papa love each other, and the love creates a baby." She said it quickly, as if it were a well-rehearsed line. "So the mama duck and papa duck create the ducklings with their love, too?"

"Yes..." Erik blinked at how smart she'd become.

"Well suppose somewhere along the way, the mama and papa duck find a duckling that isn't theirs, but is all alone..." I took over. "Do you think that if they let that duckling be with them, they're still a family?"

"You...mean like how Madame Giry adopted Auntie Christine in a way?"

"Yes, exactly. She loved Auntie Christine and wanted to take care of her, like another daughter."

"Then...I *guess* they're a family...if Madame Giry's love...*created* that space for Auntie Christine next to Auntie Meg..." She nodded slowly, glancing back at the ducks. Moments later, she looked back at us. "Are you going to adopt a baby, Mama?" Her eyes were huge again, and I lost all ability to speak.

"Janelle..." Erik slowly knelt down, pulling her into his arms. "I...we already have." His lower lip trembled, but he pushed on. "You see...before Mama and I were married, I...I found you...in the Opera House stables. I didn't want you to be alone. So Mama and I became the family you needed. We both wanted to share our love with you."

"Y–you mean, m–my mama and papa...are gone...?"

"We...we don't know, Janelle..." I sniffled, kneeling down as well. "What we do know is that we'll always love you. You will always be our little girl. And...someday, you might get to meet your mama or papa..."

"H–how will I know them...? What do I call you...?" The confusion and fear were rising in her voice.

"You can call us whatever you like, sweetheart..." I smiled softly. "As for the rest...if and when it happens, we'll figure something out. The only thing you need to think about is how much you are surrounded in love...by us and your brother and sister, all your friends, your Aunties and Madame Giry...we'll all always be there for you...I promise..."

"I–I don't want another mama and papa...I just want *us* to be a family..."

"Of course, Janelle...of course..." Erik kissed her head, and we both held her a little closer and a little longer before taking the long walk back to the Opera House.

****

  Just as predicted, Carlotta made her return appearance two opening nights later. We had just settled into Box Five when we heard a commotion from the next box over. Even before I saw the blur of fluffy pink, I knew. I quickly took Erik's hand and could feel it was already clenched. "Erik, don't let her steal our enjoyment of our daughter's performance..." I whispered. "She's not the one on stage. Don't put the limelight back on her." It took him several minutes, but he eventually was able to focus on the stage. Ironically, I was the one to keep glancing over at the former Prima Donna, watching to see any hints at all. When her eyes did widen in recognition, instinct took over. *Don't you **dare** take my little girl away!*

  "Sarah?" Erik's concerned voice snapped me out of it. "Intermission...Do you want to get some air or go backstage?" I blinked, realizing I'd missed the entire first half. *Janelle will never forgive me...*

  "B–backstage..." I bit my lip, forcing a smile for the little ones' sakes. As we made our way toward where Janelle's group was waiting, I struggled to find words. Normally at this point, I'd comment on her performance thus far. Thankfully, Erik took that upon himself while I hung back with Claire and Antoin.

  Erik had barely gotten a hug in, however, before we heard the shrill cry from behind us. Costume feathers brushed past us with such a forceful breeze they almost knocked Claire over. "It's you, isn't it? My daughter...You're taking after my footsteps after all!" Tears of joy ran down the Italian diva's face, oblivious to Janelle's confusion as she wrapped her arms around the girl tightly. Surprisingly for both Erik and I, the tears looked completely genuine, and I knew this would be harder than I thought. Once again, though, Erik's old instincts kicked in.

"Señora, unhand *my* daughter before you squeeze the last note out of her voice." His tone was cold and guarded, and I could tell he was using every ounce of strength to not lash out.

"Excuse me, but no! She is *my* little girl, and I will do as I want!"

"You—" His face was reddening. Before it could escalate further, Antoinette appeared and offered to take the children, pointing out an empty room. Not wasting any time, Erik pulled Carlotta into it, and I had to run after them to get inside before he slammed the door. "You abandoned her!" Never had I seen him this angry. Not even when I practically followed him to the lair. I expected the worst; I thought for sure she'd be her casual self, adding to his fury. I wondered how I would possibly be able to separate them. As it turned out, I didn't need to even consider it, because Carlotta's tears continued.

"I had no choice!" She sniffled before finally realizing who she was talking to. "....**YOU!** I certainly would not have left her knowing a *murderer* was to find her! I should call the police!"

"The Vicomte already had that chance, Señora, and he did not take it. Do not change the subject."

"Well if you think I'm going to leave my little girl in *your* hands, you can think again!"

"You gave up that right when you left her in the stables **of a rundown, abandoned Opera House** no less! Of all the places, you practically left her on my doorstep. Sarah and I are the only parents she has ever known, and it's a far greater love than you could ever show her!"

"At least I am not a murdering monster like you! Wait til I tell her who you really are and *then* we'll see which home is more loving!"

"You're right. I haven't told her *yet*. She's still young. What she *does* know is that I will always, *always* be there for her. That is something you cannot promise."

"Except I already told you I *had* to leave her!"

"You could have chosen an orphanage! You were *lucky* that I was even still there!"

"Lucky??" The Italian shrieked in bitter laughter. "I meant for Madame Giry to find her!"

"Why?" I surprised all three of us by speaking up, but I had to know. "Why did you have no choice?" At that, Carlotta sniffled, plopping down onto a chair. She took the handkerchief I offered before pouting.

"Her father was one of my devotees who became a close friend...He was there for me after...after my beloved Piangi was cruelly murdered..." She threw a glare at Erik before continuing. "We only wanted friendship from each other, and that's how it was for several years, with a little bit of casual flirting if either of us needed extra cheering up...We did not mean for things to go as far as they did...but, then one night, thoughts about Piangi would not go away...Arnaldo came running to console me, and," she shook her head with a sniffle, "...and the next morning, he disappeared after leaving a note. He did not want our friendship to be awkward.

"When I found out I was pregnant, I figured perhaps now I should settle down. But my public had other ideas...They wanted me to travel...do private performances. It would not be the right life for her, but I could not refuse them. They love me after all...So I did what was best for my little girl...my precious..." Even Erik could not argue with her tears then. This was no performance. He would agree that she was not that good of an actress.

"I...I'm so sorry, Carlotta...Truly..." I bit my lip. "You've been on my mind and in my prayers the moment Erik brought her to me..." I gently touched her shoulder. "Janelle...she knows that she's adopted. I'm open to letting her be introduced to you...get to know you. But the choice should be hers to make."

"Sarah, what are you saying?" Erik spoke up. "We cannot let her live a life as unpredictable as Carlotta's! What happens when the next opportunity arises?"

"Erik, she knows our love...she knows we'll always be here. But if we turn her mother away, she'll always be wondering."

"Wait!" Carlotta broke in. "Before I agree to anything...how can I trust that you will not harm her after all you did...You hate me and so how do I know you will not treat my daughter the same?" At that, Erik let out a small chuckle.

"Believe it or not, I never *hated* you. And if I really wanted to harm you, I would have. Everything I did to you was nothing more than childish pranks. You irritated me is all."

"Was killing my true love a harmless prank then?" She sniffled and glared.

"I...had my reasons. It was not just so I could take his place on stage, believe me. But in addition to disobeying me about losing weight to make the switch less noticeable, there were other factors...some of which even you were not aware of about him...things that...if you knew, would only hurt you more."

"And so you expect me to believe that you were protecting me? Don't make me laugh!"

"Believe me or not, Señora, but it is the truth nonetheless. Your daughter is precious to me and to my wife as well. I could never, ever harm her." He slowly looked down at his hands.

"Which is why I could never deny her the chance...You will go with Sarah on an outing with her. I'd insist on being present, but your time with her should be about her and not our animosity. While you may not fully trust me, Carlotta, I do not fully trust you to not steal her away only to abandon her again. She must have the final choice...Not me, not Sarah, not you. Am I clear?"

"I...suppose that is fair..." she gave a final sniffle before standing up. "May I see her now?"

"After the performance. The intermission is long past over by now." Upon that realization, we made our way back to our respective boxes, after collecting the two younger ones of course.

****

The outing with Carlotta started out as shaky. Even if I were from this time period, she and I still would have been from different worlds entirely. I would have been satisfied with a day in the park with a stop at the cafe or a bookshop. Carlotta arrived at the Opera House all ready for a day of shopping and extravagance. Seeing the tension building, Erik wisely suggested that we let Janelle decide before he planted a kiss on my lips and ushered the younger children away; I suspect that he wanted to make his escape before she started in on her dramatics. What he missed out on was to witness her agree he was right, albeit reluctantly. "Very well, *cara mia*, would you prefer the park, or would you rather pick out some nice new things?" She asked Janelle, throwing me a slight smirk for the way she worded the options.

"Actually, I'd like to go to the Charity Bazaar..."

"What?? Oh, *cara mia*, you don't understand...*those* things are all *used*! Darling, I can get you anything you want, all brand new!"

"That doesn't matter to me, Ma—" Janelle paused and glanced between the two of us. "Mother...Some of the other girls have gone to it before, and they find such wonderful things. Besides, the money goes to help those who need it..."

"...Like orphans..." Carlotta jumped several steps ahead of her daughter's train of thought, rolling her eyes in defeat. "Very well, *cara mia*...we'll go to the bazaar..." Motioning Janelle into the carriage first, she stopped me from immediately following. "I see you wasted no time in telling her everything about me..." she hissed.

"On the contrary..." I shook my head. "I thought it best to let you do that, when you're ready. It's *your* story to tell. She only knows that we'd found her...the compassion she's developed is her own, perhaps due to several of her friends being orphans and the fact that she could very well have been one of them as well."

"Hmph..." the diva sneered. "I'll tell her about me when your husband tells her about his own actions." With that, she climbed up into the carriage, leaving me to roll my eyes and let out an exasperated sigh before following her.

As we explored the various stalls at the bazaar, Carlotta initially hung back, not even bothering to feign interest in buying anything for herself. Knowing that she did have more of an eye for fashion than I did, however, I encouraged her to advise her daughter on her purchases. The tiny boost to her ego was all she needed before she was pawing through piles of items, searching for just the right pieces to accessorize and complete the dresses Janelle set her heart on getting.

At one point, Janelle and I both spotted a girl in a tattered dress eying a pair of shoes in Carlotta's hand. "Mother..?" Janelle tugged on her arm. "I don't want those shoes...let her have them..." She motioned to our audience.

"Oh but *cara mia*, there's nothing else here that goes with this dress you want..."

"She can have that too..." At that, the other girl's eyes widened.

"No....I don't have the money..." She shook her head.

"Can we get it for her then, Mother?" Janelle persisted. "You were going to buy them anyway..." Seeing the former diva's continued facial expressions of protest, she continued. "We are here to help, after all..."

"Oh, very well..." Carlotta sighed before muttering a string of Italian as she handed over the items as well as a stack of bills from her purse.

"Thank you, Mother!" Janelle beamed, throwing her arms around the bewildered Italian before presenting the girl with the gifts. Carlotta then turned her attention back to the surrounding stalls.

"I–I *must* get her *something*...I owe her..."

"Don't you see?" I touched her arm, stilling its nervous fidgeting. "You've given her something that money can't buy...the example of giving what we can to help those in need. She'll remember this long after that dress has worn down to rags. And you're spending time with her *now*. Money can't buy back lost time. Only time can make up for that. All she really needs is for you to be here for her." The former diva took several moments before she met my gaze, and when she did, her eyes were brimming with tears.

"Then...I will be here for her." Although Erik would say that she had yet to prove it, something in her shaky voice assured me that she would do her very best to keep that promise.

****

"Exactly how much longer is she going to be here...?" Meg cringed and rubbed her forehead. We were watching what was supposed to be the final dress rehearsal, but Carlotta, being Carlotta...let's just say if you thought she was overly demanding before, imagine how she was when it came to her wishes for her daughter, whether Janelle had even thought of them or not. It had already been a month; whenever we went to visit Janelle or take her on an outing, Carlotta was there, insisting on being included. What made matters worse for Erik especially was that Janelle loved the extra attention. To be sure, she still clung to the values we'd taught her, but when given the chance to sing instead of dance, she took it.

A feathery, fruit-topped hat flew past inches from my head, snapping me back. "It's all wrong!! My daughter looks best in crimson! She will not be singing under a pile of scarlet! Of course it's different, are you blind??"

"....I'll handle this..." Erik muttered, stepping from my side.

"...Erik, don't..." I reached out to stop him, but he'd already disappeared. Thankfully, he was headed for the stage and not a backdrop rope. Hat in hand, he replaced it onto Janelle's head before continuing toward the diva.

"You get away from me!" Carlotta took a step back.

"To answer your question..." I cleared my throat. "I believe she's planning on staying another month."

"Your poor, poor husband..." Meg's eyes widened.

"Oh, I know..."

"What do you think you are doing?" Panic rose in Carlotta's voice, but she stood her ground. Shreds of crimson material she'd been holding up came flying down on her head.

"If you want crimson, Señora, *you* wear it!" That did it. As he prepared to walk back toward me, she pounced. She really pounced. But of course, Erik was one step ahead of her, and so she thunked to the crimson-littered floor.

"You will be paying for this because now I am injured!"

"No one told you to try to fly..." he barely blinked, fighting back a smirk unsuccessfully. I don't know what to call the sound that emitted from her throat then. But only Erik would have the courage to keep going, and he did. By now, everyone's shock had turned to amusement. Watching them was like watching a brother and sister. The more I thought about it, the more possible it became. But, nope, I wasn't about to suggest it to either of them. It was best to leave them with no further forced connection than was already there.

"Someone should really put a stop to this..." Meg whispered.

"You've done it now because we are leaving! Janelle, I'm taking you shopping!"

"I have to rehearse...!" Janelle finally spoke up.

"You mean you *want* to rehearse in a hat that is not your color?" Carlotta blinked, genuinely shocked.

"I like it..." The little girl replied, straightening it on her head.

"I see you have a lot to learn!" Carlotta turned on her heel and stormed out, leaving a trail of Italian orders and insults. And crimson confetti. I ignored my housekeeping instincts. Slowly, Janelle picked up a piece and took off her hat, comparing the two.

"Is she right, Auntie Meg?"

"She...has a different way of thinking, sweetie. It's neither right nor wrong. All that matters is which color *you* like." After studying the two shades a little longer, Janelle looked back up.

"Could we maybe...keep the scarlet but make the feathers crimson?"

"I'll see what Bellina can do..." Meg slowly took the hat. "In the meantime, let's rehearse without the hat, alright?" Nodding in agreement, Janelle scampered back into place, and Erik made his way back over to us. I didn't know it then, but that was when the dark cloud slowly rolled in that would unsettle my stomach.

****

After Carlotta left, things quieted down to normal. We busied ourselves with lessons and picnics, and readying Antoin for the Opera House orchestra. Though he wasn't going to perform right away, the rehearsals would be his practice time. During the performances, he would then run errands for the stagehands and prop department. Eventually, he would either join the set artists and designers or the orchestra, wherever he was needed.

Carlotta did remain in touch with Janelle through letters, and one autumn day, we were greeted at the Opera House with the news that Janelle had been invited to spend Christmas in Italy. It took much persuasion, but once Erik saw how excited Janelle was at the opportunity, he begrudgingly agreed.

Upon her return after New Years, Janelle's face showed even more excitement. Carlotta would be traveling to New York in the late spring. She wanted Janelle to join her. We asked her about the opera. She said she'd still be performing and maybe return to Paris someday. She promised to keep in touch. She agreed we'd always be a family. She simply wanted to make up for lost time, which we of course understood. And so, with heavy hearts and barely hidden tears, we let her go.

    At first, it was just as if she was just at the Opera House. We tried to keep things as normal and positive as always for Claire's sake. But then, one morning I awoke to the distant sound of Erik crying, apparently from the kitchen. I slowly crept down the hallway to find him collapsed on the floor, dishes everywhere and lumpy batter all over the place. "I've watched you make them countless times...but I can't seem to..." He looked up at me, tears flooding down his red, puffy face.

    "Oh, Erik..." I bit back tears of my own at the sight; he truly was the wandering child. Silently, I threw together another batch of brownies while cleaning up at the same time. Once they were in the oven, I plopped down on the floor next to him, gently rubbing his back.

    "I–I lost her...I made her a promise the moment I found her...a–and I've lost her..."

    "You haven't lost her, my love..." I reached down and took his hand, still rubbing his back with my other one. "We both knew this day would come...It just happened sooner than we anticipated."

    "She'll ruin her...Poison her mind against me...Undo everything..."

    "That's not true. Janelle's got a good head on her shoulders. We have to believe that we raised her right. Don't sell her or yourself short."

    "How can you be so calm and sure? She's the one who brought us together...Opened my eyes...Made me feel and do things I never thought possible. It's like God gave me this light only to take it away..."

"Erik, it's not forever..." I pulled him closer. "We've had twelve years so far with her. It's only right that Carlotta gets equal time. She'll be back..If anything, we could go to New York someday. But we must give them time....Give Carlotta the chance to be the mother she wanted to be...Give Janelle the space to grow and learn from mistakes and choices...As hard as it is, Erik, we had to let her go."

"Yes, and every time I let someone go, I lose them forever!"

"That's not been true so far..." I gently caressed his face. "Christine's become a good friend, and you let *me* go, and I came back..."

"That's only because you're impossibly stubborn." He sniffed, but a small smile finally made an appearance.

"If anything, think of it as a possibility for Janelle to change *Carlotta* for the better..."

"I suppose that's possible..." He considered it. "Very possible..."

"After all," I kissed him before standing up, offering my hand. "Think of how she changed us both..."

"For the better..." Erik smiled and stood.

"For the better..." I repeated, taking the brownies out of the oven before our lips met once again.

Banishing Darkness
A Poem by Erik J. Dupree
Following the breakthrough in the lair
Before finding Janelle
~~~~~~~~~~~~~~~~~~~~

So, my darkness
We meet again
Loneliness,
I see that shame has left the candles burning
Knowing that I would return—
This is my home, after all

You three have always been my friends
Ever present
Faithful and loyal
My truest companions—
Yet, something has changed
This no longer feels like the home I've known

The comfort you three have brought me
Now no longer feels safe
You chased away the one I love
Stripped these walls of her music
Leaving me in silence
My greatest enemy

Now, you attacked another
Robbing me of her presence
Someone who's become
More of a friend than all of you combined

So here we are
Facing each other in a new light
She told me if I let you go
I will be free
To embrace my full potential

You lied to me!
Made me think that you were my destiny
All I was good for
All I was meant for
Now that I know the truth...
That I was created out of love
That I have a purpose
And am not some random mistake
To be cast aside and forgotten
I see now that there's no room for you
In my life

So get out of here, shame!
Despite all the things I've done
You no longer shall define me
Nor shall you hold me back

Your chains have been shattered
Never again will I be your prisoner
My debts have been paid for
My soul set free
By the Only One
Who has the right to condemn me
He was the One I offended
And He chooses to forgive
Mercy and Grace
Have taken your place
Redeemed
Is how I shall be defined evermore.

So go away, Loneliness!
The truth is I have never been alone!
All this time
I've been within His Sight
And in His Hand—
He's protected me
Giving me every single breath
So that I would eventually see.
I no longer have to settle
For you as my only companion
On the contrary
My Truest Friend has been here
Waiting
Ever patient

Ever constant
Ever faithful
And the one who showed Him to me
Has become closer than you've ever been
Fighting you before I knew you were my enemy
She is no longer here
But I'll not let you win this time
I'll not stay here for long
Her friendship
And the presence of the Holy Spirit
Have taken your place
There's no room for you anymore

And oh, darkness, how I loathe you!
Do not think I've forgotten to address you
No, I've saved you for last with good reason.
You deceived me more than the others
Cloaking me in a blanket of fear
Pretending I'd be safe in your care
Oh, but no...No!!
You attacked the innocents!
Invading their sleep with nightmares
Haunting their imaginations by day with your shadows.
Recruiting me into your disgusting plan!
No more!
I am no longer your puppet
You cannot use me for your amusement anymore!

I BANISH YOU, DARKNESS!
*I banish you from this place
Just as you banished her!
Every candle I light
Makes you smaller...weaker....
And where candles won't reach
His Light will flood every corner within.
See, I believed you, darkness
I believed that light serves only to blind
Or to reveal secrets I thought were best hidden
Oh, how wrong we both were!
For when we reject the Light
We reject the warmth it brings!
When we allow it to reveal the truth
We allow ourselves to begin to heal*
SO GET OUT OF HERE DARKNESS!
DEPART FROM ME FOREVER!
*I know you no longer as my friend
You, darkness, are the enemy.*
YOU HAVE BEEN REPLACED
*By a Light that gives warmth and hope
A brand new beginning
A world of possibilities
That neither shame,
Nor loneliness,
Nor darkness
Shall ever hold me back from exploring.*

Snapshots:
Bonus scenes and little moments never forgotten

1

A nearby bird sang to welcome the day about an hour before the sun was due to rise, seeming to know that I was humming my own tune as I stirred the contents of the saucepan in front of me. I allowed my mind to wander, reliving the night before as breakfast simmered. Just then, tender yet strong arms slid around my robed waist from behind as his lips found their rest against my neck. "Breakfast smells delightful..." He whispered.

"It's only oatmeal with dried berries and almonds..." I giggled dismissively. "I've made it countless times before..." I closed my eyes as he continued to leave trails of kisses along my neck and earlobe, and I felt him wrap his hand around mine on the spoon's handle, helping me stir.

"This morning is special..." He reasoned, moving the saucepan off of the heat.

"Indeed it is..." I nodded, leaning back against him. "I was going to surprise you by bringing this to you with a few other things..."

"Oh? Well, my dear, do forgive me for spoiling your fun..." He teased sarcastically. "I'll get right back to bed...!" He started to pull away, but that only allowed me to turn around and wrap my own arms around him.

"I'm glad you're feeling up to being back on your feet, my love...We can just as easily share this meal anywhere you'd like..."

"Perhaps the sofa, then...I've spent enough time in that bedroom...for now anyways..." He smirked, sending red heat to my cheeks.

"The sofa it is then..." I pecked his jaw and stepped away before breakfast could be forgotten entirely. He seemed to recognize the cue as he made himself comfortable on the sofa, watching me put the finishing touches on the meal.

"I do have a confession, my dear..." He finally spoke up as I set the tray down on the coffee table. Once I was settled, I looked at him to continue. "I was already up earlier...Janelle had been crying. When I saw you curled up in my arms beside me, I hated to leave you...but I knew if she continued, you'd be disturbed and have to leave *me*...You'd done more than your fair share already..."

"I must have really been out to not notice your absence, however brief it might have been..." I unwrapped the basket of pastries and handed him one.

"Have you forgotten that being sneaky is second-nature to me?" He raised an eyebrow as he took a bite.

"Mm…That's very true…I'll have to start sleeping with one eye open…" I giggled.

"And I'll just sneak up on the eye that's closed…" He retorted with a growl.

"You're impossible!" I playfully hit his arm, but then he caught my hand and brought its knuckles to his lips.

"Oh no, my dear….you're the impossible one…I still can't get over any of this, let alone all of it…It would still feel a dream, were I not holding you now…"

"Believe me, the feeling's mutual…" I let myself fall against him. Silence surrounded us then, as we fed each other between kisses and sighs of contentment.

2

"Did you hear something…?" I mumbled, rolling over to face my husband in the darkness.

"Only you…" He muttered with a trace of lightheartedness as he sat up against the headboard, pulling me close.

"No…I thought for sure I heard something just outside the window…" At that, I felt him tense with fresh alertness; by now I'd grown used to the typical nighttime noises of the countryside, and so for something to break through my slumber, it could not be ignored.

"I'll take a look…" He pecked my head before swinging his legs over the side of the mattress. "Why don't you check on Janelle and Antoin? Stay there until I return..?"

"Good idea…" I nodded and slowly got up. At the door, I paused and turned around. "Be careful?"

"Madame Dupree…" His voice smirked in the darkness, and then his arms were wrapping themselves around me reassuringly. "Just whom do you think you are talking to?"

"Of course…how silly of me…" I allowed myself to giggle a bit as our lips met. He held me for a few moments longer before taking a step back.

"We'll continue this discussion when I return…Clearly you need a reminder…" He growled slightly. "Now, don't wake the children if they aren't aware of any noises. Just wait for me there…"

"Right…" I nodded, giving his hands one more squeeze before silently making my way to the next room.

Relief swept over and through me as I heard the reassuring sound of both our children's soft, even breaths; I likened it to a sort of lullaby to a concerned mother's anxious ears. Perhaps, Erik had figured I needed it more than they needed my presence at that time. I smiled at the thought of childhood dreams dancing through their innocent minds, slowly lowering myself to the rocking chair.

I must have dozed off, because the next thing I remember, a tiny bundle of fur was brushing against my hands as it was lowered onto my lap. Blinking in shock and sleepiness, my fingers immediately recognized the shape of a kitten as the tiniest 'mew' broke the silence. "There's your intruder…" Erik knelt down beside the chair then, whispering yet another smirk.

"Oh…!" I bit my lip, gently stroking the kitten's head.

"Come into the kitchen…" My husband carefully helped me up, and we slipped out of the room to leave our children to their dreams.

"How do you suppose I heard such a tiny sound?" I wondered aloud, holding the kitten to my chest and letting it curl up in my hand.

"I asked myself the same question…" He chuckled, lighting a couple of lamps before fixing a dish for our little visitor. "But then I remembered all you said about your cat back in your time…Perhaps it was a sort of mothering instinct…"

"I do miss her…" I nodded slightly, forcing myself to focus on the kitten in my hand instead of the memories. "This one's a calico as well…"

"If memory serves me correctly, you put Patches in one of your stories…as Carmella…?"

"I did…" I blinked in astonishment. "I can't believe you remembered that…!"

"Of course…As perplexing as your ideas were at the time, they still stayed with me." Silence fell as we tended to the kitten's needs, allowing my thoughts time to wander.

"Was…she alone?" I finally thought to ask.

"As far as I could tell…" He nodded with a sigh. "I'll keep my eyes and ears out the next several days, just in case." When little Carmella finally had her fill and curled up against my chest, I knew she would be no mere visitor. Erik silently agreed to my unspoken decision by gently scratching behind her ear before leading us both back to bed.

The cool saltwater sent a chill up my spine as I gingerly waded into it–a stark contrast to the sun-baked sand not even an inch behind me. Rather than flinch, however, I closed my eyes with a sigh of relief. Where I was from, I'd had my pick of streams, rivers, and lakes to dip my feet into on any given day, and so I relished the sensation completely. To be sure, we now lived by a river, and yet so few were the opportunities to spend an entire day of recreation by it and in it. This particular summer day, however, the DeChagneys had generously treated the entire opera house and their families to a day at the beach in Deauville; a belated celebration of the reconstruction. Erik had at first been somewhat reluctant to take part in such a large-scale social event with very little, if any, hiding places available, but our children's enthusiasm pulled him into agreement.

Water splashed up my legs, soaking the bottoms of my bathing suit before I was quite ready, stealing me back into the present as Erik raced Gustaave, Janelle, and Antoin into the waves with their buckets, five-year-old Claire trying to keep up. Their eagerness nearly knocked me off-balance, but I quickly recovered with a laugh at my husband's excitement. This had been yet another motivation I'd suggested to ease his mind about the outing, and I was pleased to see him taking me up on it. The four of them dipped their pails into the water before running back to where he was showing them how to build a fortress of sand rather than the simpler castles other children were working on. "Just no tunnels!" I called after him with a laugh, catching Claire before she fell from the sudden change of direction.

"Wait for me!" She barely acknowledged my help before scampering towards them, Meg's son Henri taking it upon his six-year-old self to take her by hand the rest of the way so he, too, could join.

"It's amazing to see how much they've all grown..." Christine voiced my impending observation as she and Meg approached me.

"Yes..." I nodded with a happy sigh, looking past the two honorary sisters to the now teenaged Marguerite and Lottie DeChagney, setting their attentions albeit shyly on two young men from the orchestra.

"It won't be long now..." The Vicomptess echoed my sigh, bringing her hand up to her forehead with a small giggle. "And yet they have much still to learn..."

"As did we all...a good portion of it the hard way..." I added, my smile fading.

"Oh, but look where it brought us!" Meg interrupted our laments, motioning back toward where the children were now piling on top of Erik, trying to bury him in the remains of one of the fortress walls that had apparently collapsed from too much water. "Each one of them is the result of lessons learned *from* those mistakes. We can share our wisdom, but it's up to them to accept it either now or after they've stumbled themselves."

"That's very true…" I nodded, my smile returning.

"Now then, should we go rescue your husband?" Christine giggled.

"What, and spoil the children's fun?" I gasped jokingly, bending down to grab a fistful of mud before running over to the fort.

Later on, Erik and I sat with the DeChagneys, Antoinette, and Meg while Robert and some of the other men led the older children on a seashell hunt to allow the younger ones to nap. As we settled into the quiet in between conversations, Erik chose to pull out his drawing pad and pastel set; he never went on any sort of journey without some way of capturing the sights he found to be inspirational. I rested my chin on his shoulder, watching him blend colors only an eye as practiced as his own could pick up on. So lost were we both in the work he was creating that we just about forgot our nearby surroundings. "You truly are an artist, Erik…" Christine's voice pierced the silence, startling us both. As Erik glanced her way, she continued her observation. "In all those years, I don't think I ever saw you work on any art pieces…I only saw the finished pictures…"

"No, I don't suppose you did…" Erik blinked at the realization, as if he'd been suddenly awakened from a nap. He pondered his next words for several moments before releasing a sigh. "I would have loved for you to have at least one of those drawings, if they'd only not been destroyed…"

"That's an easy fix…" Antoinette motioned to the blank pages underneath his current drawing.

"Of course..!" Fresh inspiration dissolved his look of regret as he flipped to a new page. By the time we readied to leave the beach in the early evening, Erik had gifted a family portrait to both couples, and a mother and daughter portrait to Antoinette. For me, he'd captured our children's wonder and curiosity as they examined shells along the waterline—oceanside treasures which they'd slipped into mine and Erik's hands to be cherished along with the memories made that day.

Phantom of the Sea

*****PROLOGUE*****

    Years have passed since Erik invaded the resort, and we've gotten much older. It was so surreal watching *my* history pass before my eyes as the present...So many events I'd learned about, so many more I hadn't even heard of.

    Our children grew up of course, and had lives of their own. Antoin became quite the architect, building a gallery in Paris to display both his and Erik's works of art. Unlike most artists who only get appreciated after death, the two of them were blessed enough to have quite a few commissions requested of them at a steady flow.

    As for Claire, she left home around the age of sixteen, becoming a housekeeper and companion to Antoinette when the Opera House became too much for her. There, she fell in love with Meg's oldest son, Henri. Antoin was more than happy to build them a cottage near Antoinette so that Claire could still keep up with her duties at both homes.

    And then, there was Janelle. As we'd both hoped, she did indeed return to France for about five years once she was old enough to travel alone. Yet she did not travel alone for long; as a matter of fact, she arrived in the company of a sailor who'd taken it upon himself to act as an escort and bodyguard. Though we were initially apprehensive of his line of work and the reputation that comes with it, Samuel proved himself to be quite the gentleman.

    In the time it took them to be engaged and married, Janelle graced the Opera House stage with her presence once again. Erik all but burst into tears when he heard her voice; she'd remembered each lesson and sang with every bit of talent he knew she'd always had the potential to achieve. What's more, despite her mother's personality and mistakes, Janelle also remained true to the values Meg, Antoinette, and I had instilled in her. She was always the first to comfort and encourage anyone who showed stage fright or self-doubt, dancing or singing along with them until they could do it on their own. It would be an understatement to say that we were all very proud of her.

After a while, however, word got back to them about a sudden illness coming over Carlotta. Her position in the show she'd been a part of was now left open, and the producers felt that only Janelle was fit for it. Only after it was ensured that Samuel would find employment in the harbor did they agree to move back to New York, taking their children, Lydia and Joseph, and their nanny with them. We were of course a little heartbroken, but once again we vowed to travel there for a visit someday.

****

One morning, I awoke to find Erik practically towering over me from his chair beside the bed, only a drawing tablet separating us. His brow was furrowed in deep concentration as he moved the charcoal around, smudging effortlessly as he went. I so loved to watch him work; his artistic focus was one of many qualities of his that I deeply admired. When he finally became aware of the fact that I was awake, his eyes sparkled and danced, his smile smoothing his wrinkles but for a moment. "Don't move....close your eyes and go back to sleep..."

"Don't tell me you're doing another one of me...! You've done so many already..!"

"Not like this one. Now shh...do as I say..." Despite the slight growl in his voice, I couldn't help but detect the slightest return of his smile. Rolling my eyes, I obliged his wishes, giggling inwardly.

"There!" He finally exclaimed triumphantly several minutes later. "My beautiful, adorable, angel of a wife..."

"Oh come on...adorable?" I scoffed, fixing my braid. Gray streaks now outnumbered the former brown hue my hair once held, and the remainder of his hair was now snowy white. Because it had thinned so much, he normally wore a wig of the same shade. Aside from the hair color and inevitable wrinkles, the two decades of continued hard work this time period required kept him as fit as Antoin. That energy was spent not only maintaining the house and land, but also leading in the upkeep of the village church. On Sundays, of course, he played the organ. It was a wonder he found any time at all to work on his art.

"Yes, adorable." He stopped my hand, placing the finished drawing in my lap before gently working on my hair himself, brushing his lips against my cheek. "And angelic...did I mention that?"

"You did..." I studied the drawing. "You mean to say that I'm only angelic when I'm sleeping?" I teased.

"Precisely..." He met my dig evenly, with a smirk plastered on his face. The pillow I flung at him only caused it to grow as he easily ducked out of the way, not missing a beat with my hair. "Need I say more?"

"You're up early..." I changed the subject. "And far too cheerful. What's going on?"

"Madame Dupree...you really mean to tell me that you've forgotten your own anniversary?" He raised an eyebrow, the smirk still spreading. I could have melted then. That expression always did me in, especially paired with the reminder that he'd adopted the last name I'd given him in my stories.

"Of course not!" I gasped dramatically. "But you normally wait until supper to shower me with gifts..."

"Well then it's high time I surprise you, isn't it?" He chuckled, finishing my hair before pulling me close. "That drawing is the first..."

"You never cease to amaze me..." I turned to kiss him. "But now how am I supposed to wake you up with breakfast in bed?" I jokingly pouted.

"Oh! My dear, do forgive me!" He laughed his way under the covers, propping himself up against the headboard. "Ready when you are, my lovely wife!" I giggled at his excitement as I stood up, bending down to trace his scars with my lips.

"You impossible dream, you..." I giggled softly, caressing his face.

"Mm...do impossible dreams get hungry?" He pulled back just enough out of my reach so that I could see his playful smirk had returned.

"Oh! My dear, do forgive me!" Throwing his words back at him like a verbal pillow, I reluctantly went to the kitchen.

The day went on with similar banter, halting only during the short visits from Antoin, Claire, and Henri. Supper had just concluded when a messenger arrived for Erik. "Ah...perfect timing..." Taking the envelope, he thanked the messenger before returning to the kitchen table.

"Now what do you have up your sleeve?" I raised an eyebrow. Every year he did this, insisting that I need not attempt to match the amount of gifts I received, and that my love was enough of a gift. Still, I'd always managed to cook his favorite dishes, write him a poem, or even present him with a few photographs once I'd gotten the hang of the new—I mean—old technology of the cameras of that time. It certainly made me both miss my digital camera as well as appreciate all the work that went into, er, developing them.

"My arm, if you must know..." Erik smirked, handing me the envelope. I slowly opened it, revealing two ocean liner tickets and a note explaining that Erik would be playing the piano for Sunday services and a few dinners and concerts during the voyage late the following spring to—

"New York!" I grinned.

"Yes! The reverend arranged everything, as he will also be on board. It's high time we had that honeymoon we missed out on, as well as seeing Janelle and all the sights..." I pounced before he could continue, thunking us both to the floor. Laughing, he pulled me all the closer. "As I said...you're adorable, and you always will be, no matter the age..."

"And angelic?" I smirked against his lips.

"Only when you're sleeping..." He growled.

****

#####*ONE*#####

No matter how many times I reminded myself that *The Sapphire* was not *Titanic* and that there were still seven years until the infamous disaster would take place, my stomach was still doing flip flops from the moment we stepped out of the carriage onto the docks. Her trim and hull were painted a shade of blue to match her name, and in the morning light, she glistened just like the gem she was named after. Her beauty served as more than a distraction from my nerves; I was so awestruck that Erik had to press my bag's handle against my fingers before I remembered we were actually there. The stewards were already approaching the gangplank with our trunks. We'd be at sea for about a week each way, with two months in America in between. Antoin had agreed to watch over our property in our absence; he said it always gave him the most inspiration for his art. I also suspected it was to keep his mind off of the recent break to his longtime courtship with one of his devotees. He'd found out the hard way that she'd been merely interested in his fame and fortune; she'd thrown a fit when he hit a block on a commission and had to refund the money. Erik and I had encouraged him of course, but now he needed time and space to himself.

Following Erik onboard, I was once again brought back to the present. Despite the crowd of passengers and crew, my eyes still fell on countless pieces of decor which continued the blue and white color scheme. With that combination being among my favorites, I quickly fell in love with each piece, whether landscape painting, miniature statue, or even the way the bottoms of the grand staircase banisters were carved.

As part of the band, we'd been given a stateroom in second class. Before I could even set down my small bag, Erik was maneuvering the furniture and bunk mattresses to make it into a double bed on the floor. "You'll remember to put all that back before we go ashore, right?" I raised an eyebrow, reminded of some of the instances at the resort where we'd have to put furniture back that the guests moved around. I refused to make more work than necessary.

"Of course!" He promised, already unpacking and completely oblivious to just how cramped the room now was. There was no use mentioning it though, I reminded myself with a smile. This was to be our honeymoon after all, and to spend it on separate bunks would only be a repeat of our wedding night. Instead, I crawled across the long, built-in couch and peered out the porthole.

It wouldn't be long before the open sea replaced the docks in view, and so I wanted to take in as much of the sight before me as I could. Although it wasn't Paris, the hustle and bustle brought to mind all my favorite shops; I always thought how fitting it was to have a florist, chocolatier and bakery, and a bookshop all adjacent to each other. So many times after a quarrel or even when one of his artistic moods escalated too much for his comfort, Erik would storm off into town, only to return with an armload of parcels from every one of those shops. The sight always gave me such amusement that I couldn't not apologize or forgive him. Sometimes I wondered if he invented the arguments just to have an excuse to buy me such things; after all, I always shared the sweets as we took turns reading to each other long into the night.

"Would you care to accompany me to the first rehearsal?" His request caused me to jump a bit, pulling me from my thoughts.

"I'd love to! Would the others mind though?"

"What, to play for a beauty such as yourself? Certainly not!" He planted a soft but determined kiss upon my temple. "And if they do, they'll have me to deal with!"

"Should I speak to the captain about removing all the chandeliers?" I raised an eyebrow. Enough time had passed that I could tease him about it, though I still made sure such digs were few and far between. His response was to cause me to squeak suddenly.

"You'll pay more for that later…" He met my giggle with a growl, his eyes still dancing.

****

For the next day or so, aside from rehearsals and one dinner performance, Erik was content to stay in the cabin. After all these years, he still wasn't entirely comfortable socializing beyond church or the occasional family or small-scale community event. He no longer wore masks; even if he hadn't left the one he had been wearing behind at the resort, I'd convinced him that people would get used to his scars if he gave them enough time and opportunity to. Even so, he preferred to sit at the church organ with his back to the congregation, and now, here on *The Sapphire*, he ensured that the piano was turned so that only his left side was facing the audience. I didn't argue. I was simply content with the fact that he was up there, performing. I could tell he enjoyed it, too; even with the 'new-fangled' ragtime pieces some of the American passengers requested, he put as much heart into them as if he were playing the violin back home.

Our first night, he encouraged me to take a little stroll before bed, sensing accurately that I needed and wanted that quiet, peaceful time outdoors. I used that hour simply admiring the colors of sunset, using my camera a few times to capture silhouettes of a few couples but mostly silently praying. The second night, he decided to join me, giving the excuse that he had a dance to play for soon anyway, but I could tell he enjoyed the fresh ocean air as much as I did. At one point, we quietly but simultaneously rested our elbows on the railing, as if we'd planned it. "Chocolate for your thoughts?" He finally spoke up after several moments, holding a wrapped candy in front of me.

"Oh, everything and nothing..." I giggled softly, taking it.

"I assume, then, that your muse was productive today in the library?" He knew me all too well.

"Very..." I admitted with a small laugh. "And then I got to thinking ahead...all these 'what ifs' about my family coming across these pages someday and figuring out that it's me behind them..."

"I see..." He gently squeezed my hand. Despite everything, especially how much I loved being here and loved Erik and our family, there were many moments when I'd remember all I'd left behind. "What would you tell them, if you could?"

"That I was alright...No...more than alright..." I smiled up into his eyes. "That I'm happy and in love...and that I think of them often..."

"Perhaps we could leave something that they'd be sure to find..." He moved his fingers through my hair. "We don't have to spend all of the two months in New York..."

"I'd love that!" I grinned, kissing him excitedly.

"Then we shall..." He returned the kiss, adding a second. "For now, we should change for the dance..."

"So you *did* have time to go back to the cabin!" I nudged him with a smirk.

"And miss this lovely walk with even lovelier company?" His eyes widened defensively.

"You're too much..." I lightly hit his arm.
"Oh, but you love me all the same! You just said as much!"
"That I do...very much so..." We shared a third and fourth silent exchange before returning inside.

Although the size of the band was small, music filled the ballroom, surrounding and moving through and between the crowd of dancing couples. Even Erik couldn't keep from all but dancing on the piano bench, and I couldn't help but giggle as I watched from the side. During the pieces with more upbeat tempos, I clapped or swayed in my chair, and for the slower tunes I found myself leaning back or against the wall, rarely taking my gaze off of the man I loved. So lost was I in the atmosphere of everything that I didn't even notice my eyes had closed until I felt a familiar hand touch my shoulder. Blinking, I turned my head to see Erik standing next to me. "Shouldn't you be up there..?" I pointed toward the stage.

"Not when I wrote this piece specifically for us to dance to. No piano needed..." His eyes were already dancing ahead of us, and I let him help me to my feet. Snuggling into him, I was for once thankful that he preferred sticking to the shadows. Very few couples were moving as close together as us. Closing my eyes again, I completely surrendered to every step he led us in. Nothing fancy, just simply turning and swaying to the music, listening as he ever so softly hummed along while his heartbeat seemed to be keeping in time to the rhythm.

Before I knew it, he was gently caressing my face, signifying the end of the number and beckoning my eyes to flutter open. "My dear, you're falling asleep..." His eyes shone with concern.

"Am I?" I blinked some more. "I suppose...Especially here in your arms where I'm most comfortable...feel the most safe..."

"I kept you awake far too late last night, what with it being our official honeymoon and all..."

"I'm not complaining, love..." I smirked slightly, causing him to chuckle.

"Even so, you'd best head back to the cabin.... Get a head start on sleep so that I don't disturb you when I turn in..."

"Very well..." I sighed, refusing to admit just how right he was. The slightest yawn betrayed me, however. He brought me to the ballroom door, forcing himself to stop from walking the entire way as I could sense his heart wanted to do. As we kissed, he let his lips linger, as if we'd just come to the end of a date, stealing every precious moment we could.

"Good night, my beautiful, adorable wife..." His fingers traced my cheek and jawline before he brushed his index finger against my lower lip.

"I love you..." I pecked his finger before a second yawn escaped. Motioning to a steward, he told him our cabin number before reluctantly releasing my arm. The short walk seemed like a blur. I don't recall thanking the steward, nor if I changed into my nightgown or even took off my glasses.

I only recall dreaming I was back in my time, overhearing university students setting off fireworks. I opened my eyes, ready to have Erik put a stop to them. But he had yet to return. And the boom was real. And then, there was a creaking sound at the foot of the mattresses. I sat up on my elbow, barely able to block my head from the falling dressing table mirror as the table slammed onto my lower body. I didn't realize I was screaming until the cabin door flew off of its hinges. Flickering light flooded the cabin, and the more I studied it, the more it looked like flames instead of the electric lights along the corridor, the shadows dancing on the wall. "Sarah!" Erik's panicked yell forced my attention to his silhouetted form now filling the doorway. Not waiting for me to respond, he dropped to his knees beside me. I felt the weight of the mirror being lifted off of my arms and face before he turned his attention and energy to the dressing table. Using every ounce of his strength, he rose to his feet, picking up the set of drawers as he went. Smoke filled the room as I watched him hurl the dressing table against the porthole, the window glass shattering around it. Cold, fresh air rushed in, relieving the effects of the smoke just enough.

"E–Erik...I can't move my legs..." I whimpered, realizing only then that I was crying.

"Hold on tight...Bury your face against me..." He coughed out the instructions, gently but swiftly lifting me into his arms. Hold tight I did, because Erik then sped down the corridors, flames licking the air around us as their heat added to the stinging pain surging through me. I buried my face against him all the more out of total fear. Cold air finally enveloped us again, indicating that we were safely outside. It was only when I felt raindrops hitting me that I lifted my gaze. Everywhere I turned my head, passengers were scurrying onto the lifeboats as fast as the crew could lower them into the water.

Erik set me down then, just long enough to wrap his jacket around me and examine my face. At that moment, his eyes widened and then fell. "No...not you too..." he moaned. Before he could explain, panic broke out at the lifeboat nearest to us. We both looked to see that the crewman had collapsed, and now the lifeboat was dangling at a dangerous angle for the passengers inside. Next thing I knew, Erik had crossed the deck, grabbing the broken chains. The crowd fell silent, just for a moment, as they realized they'd be safe. Gripping the chains with everything he had, he helped the rest of the waiting passengers into the boat before a few men stepped forward to help him lower it. Once he made sure everyone knew to move to the next boats, he returned to my side.

"Erik..." I managed a whisper around the lump in my throat that was screaming in pain.

"Shh...don't try to speak..." Ripping off his shirt, he gently bandaged my face as best as he could, though I still felt warm blood trickle down onto my neck. A steward came over then, handing us blankets and lifebelts.

"We've got to get her onto a boat..."

"Us." I managed to correct him assertively. "I'm not leaving my husband behind." The uniformed man studied us for a few moments before seemingly realizing we meant it.

"Very well...follow me." Silently, he led us to a boat a little ways away, where only a few passengers had thought to line up so far. Only when Erik and I had settled into our seats did I allow the rocking motion to lull me to sleep once again.

****

#####*TWO*#####

Pain.

Stinging pain surged up and down my arm with such sharpness that I felt my hand twitch. Gentle fingers wrapped around it, the pain subsiding immediately. I knew those hands....that touch...

Opening my eyes, I was disappointed to see a thick white cloud blocking him from view. *I must be dreaming then...* A faint whimper flew past my lips. "S–Sarah...you're awake..!"

"A–am I an angel...?" I managed to mumble, though a corner of my mouth seemed to be glued shut.

"You were..." I could hear the smile in his voice....imagine the sparkle in his eyes behind the tears. "You were my angelic sleeping beauty for two days, my dear...almost three.." I felt his hand move across my face, but something was wrong. There seemed to be a barrier. Frowning, I attempted to shake it off. "Oh, my dear...Y–you can't... We can't remove the bandages...not yet..." Just like that, the dancing eyes in his voice were gone. Instead, I felt the mattress sag as he lowered himself to it next to me, ever so carefully pulling me close. His hands continued the soothing motion against my face. "The mirror...it cut you deeply in many places. Y–you needed stitches...they will heal...but scar..." His voice grew shakier with every word. "A–and your leg was broken from the dressing table...I–I should have gone back with you...brought you elsewhere..."

"Erik, don't...don't you dare blame yourself..." I reached up as best as I could to his face, ignoring the sting's return. "You didn't know..." Silence fell between us to allow for our tears to run their course, mine from sheer frustration that I couldn't see him or kiss his tears away.

Eventually, he was able to explain that one of the ship's boilers had exploded, causing the fire. Much of the crew and passengers had been lost, but those who had survived had rowed the lifeboats to a small group of islands, where the inhabitants ensured that our needs would be taken care of and another ship would be provided. "They receive shipments every month," he went on, "Once they're able to wire the next one, they'll be able to determine whether they can take passengers or arrange for a different one that can. In the meantime, you'll be able to recover enough to make the voyage back home..."

"Home? What about Janelle?"

"I...didn't think you'd be up to it after—"

"We've made it this far, love..." I snuggled closer, feeling exhaustion setting in again.

"As long as you're sure..." He seemed to know when my eyelids grew too heavy. "Don't go to sleep just yet...You need nourishment..." He left the bed then, his footsteps crossing the room and back again. Settling once more by my side, he pressed a cup to my lips, cool water trickling into my mouth. I must have caused him to make five trips across the room for more water, and then he was gone longer, returning with a large mug of hot broth. Only after I'd finished the very last drop did he allow me to settle back on the pillows, his soft humming barely needed for me to drift off to sleep once again.

****

The bandages on my face were removed the next afternoon, and as soon as it was confirmed that I could see, I requested a mirror. At first, Erik tried to stop the doctor from complying, arguing with me that it wasn't important, and if I did see, the scars would only deepen. "Erik, I understand where you're coming from, believe me. But I'm going to see it eventually, and I'd rather it be as soon as possible and on my terms so that I can get used to it. Please..." I rested my good hand on his; my right arm was still bandaged from my shoulder all the way down to the fingertips. He let out a frustrated sigh, leaving my side to glare out the window. Silently, I motioned for the mirror to be brought over. Taking a deep breath, I opened my eyes to face the reflection.

A jagged row of stitches led from the corner of my mouth to just below my earlobe, and a second one of equal length and thickness went from the left side of my eyebrow to my slightly shaved back hairline. Smaller cuts were spread out from my nose to my ear, my cheek almost completely covered where the glass had broken around my arm when I'd tried to shield myself. My glasses were also different; it was explained that my other ones had been damaged beyond repair, leaving bruises and further cuts around my eyes that had now almost healed. "You lost much blood...Your husband gave you some of his..." At that new information, I turned to look at Erik. His back was still turned to me, his shoulders slumped.

"Erik..." Before I could say anymore, he whirled around, tears streaming down his face.

"I...I tried to give you more...I-I tried to get them to use skin from my face to cover...Th–there's a fairly new procedure I–I read about...a–and...I thought–"

"Y–you were...willing to further scar..." I blinked back my own tears then, the weight of his willingness crashing over me. He'd been willing to further scar his own face.

"Th–they...said it wasn't necessary..." He sniffled, glaring at the doctor.

"Well they're right..." I motioned him over, taking his hand. "I don't need masks, nor do I want them. Unless you can look me in the eyes and tell me I'm any less beautiful or loved by you..."

"Sarah, of course not! It's just–"

"Erik, it doesn't matter to me. These things never did, you know that!"

"I–it's different when it happens to yourself..." He pouted defiantly.

"Perhaps..." I caressed the back of his hand with my thumb. "But these scars serve as a reminder...that I survived...I was stronger...They're a reminder of your love...your sacrifice...I know I don't need one, but I have it anyway...Physical, undeniable proof. And I'm no less happy." His tears fell all the more then, and I pulled him into as tight a hug as I dared.

****

A couple mornings later, I was woken up by a thorny stem being gently placed in my hand. "Erik...what–?" I slowly sat up, the darkness momentarily making me think that the bandages over my eyes had returned.

"Shh...yes, I know, the sun has yet to rise. We've got plenty of time..." Though I couldn't see him, I heard him approach the bed, creaking wheels accompanying his footsteps. With all the years he'd spent in hiding, he still didn't need any light in order to see or move around, even in a strange room. I, on the other hand, was helpless.

"Time for what...?" I knew what mood he was in, and therefore how useless it was to ask any questions.

"You'll see..." I felt his arms wrap around me then, gently turning me until my good leg dangled over the edge of the bed.

"Erik, you know I can't–" I squeaked.

"It's called a wheelchair. Surely you know about these things..." Despite my confusion, I was glad to hear the lightheartedness in his voice once again. The days between our argument and now had been somewhat silent, our conversations more abrupt and informative than anything else. It was as if he was waiting for me to change my mind about my scars...waiting for me to realize the permanence of the situation. But if anything, I was all the more determined to prove him wrong, in the most loving way possible of course. I simply avoided the subject at all cost.

"Yaaah!" The surge of pain as he placed me in the wheelchair snapped me back to reality.

"...Sorry..." I could tell he was biting his lip sheepishly. "I...at least we know you're not paralyzed...?"

"I suppose I cannot argue with that..." I muttered with a sigh, shifting ever so carefully into a more comfortable position. Pausing only to layer blankets on top of me, he wheeled me forward, through a set of double doors and onto a balcony. The weathered wood squeaked underneath us, reminiscent of an old five-and-dime I frequented during my childhood. As we reached the railing, my eyes quickly fell on the horizon, where the very first hint of dawn was rising up. This was so rare and so special, as we typically only made a point to catch the sunrise on Easter Sunday; it was a tradition not practiced here, but one I carried over from my time.

"I thought perhaps a day of fresh air and exploration would do you good..." Erik brought a chair over to my side.

"It already is..." I smiled, taking his hand. In silence, we watched the light melt the shadows away, bringing into view the rocky but mossy coastline. The cliffs reminded me of pictures I'd seen of Scotland. The building where we were was on a shallower hill, the docks and even a beach almost directly below us. All the lifeboats were still there, and for a moment, I was brought back to that disastrous night. Even now, I could smell the smoke and melting steel, see the flames through stinging eyes, hear the chaos and heartbreak. Sensing my coming tears, Erik rose to his feet and wheeled me around the corner to a long set of stairs. "...You can't be seri–***OUS***!!" I screeched as he lifted me, wheelchair and all, and carried me down the flight of stairs without so much as a grunt. I would have hit his arm, if he'd given me the chance. Smartly, however, he remained behind the chair, wheeling me towards a flower garden. Rose bushes of different colors sat in each corner, with a pathway leading directly up the middle, past benches surrounded by green leaves and brightly colored petals. At the end of the garden, the path continued into a small, wooded area.

"You'll want us to take lunch in there..." He stopped us in front of the last bench, sitting down next to me with a secretive smirk.

"Oh?" I raised my eyebrow.

"You'll see why..." His smirk grew. "For now, I borrowed the doctor's Bible. I thought we might read from the Psalms this morning. It's the perfect setting for it..." He reached into his cloak pocket, pulling out the volume.

"I'd love that..." I grinned. "Could we start with–"

"The thirteenth? But of course, my dear..." He was already flipping to my favorite Psalm, though I didn't even need to glance at the page to recall the words. "In fact, I was hoping to hear you sing it..." His suggestion made me smile all the more; a fairly local group from my time had put the passage to music. It was how I'd managed to memorize it so easily.

"How long, O Lord,
Will You forget me, forever?
How long will You hide Your Face from me?
How long must I wrestle with my thoughts
And every day have sorrow in my heart?
How long will my enemies
Triumph over me?" Erik took my hands then, the words being so personal to his past. His voice joined mine then as the Psalm continued.

"Look on me and answer,
O Lord, my God!
Give light to my eyes
Or I will sleep in death!
My enemies will say, 'I defeated you,'
And my foes will rejoice when I fall!" Our voices grew in volume as we sang the joyful twist in mood.

"But I trust in Your unfailing Love!
I rejoice because You've rescued me!
I will sing to the Lord
For He's been good to me..." Soft clapping interrupted the silence that followed, and I opened my eyes to see a young woman standing near the edge of the wood, watching us.

"That was beautiful, Monsieur...Madame..."

"Thank you..." Erik recovered his voice first. "I apologize for disturbing your morning stroll..."

"Oh, not at all!" The woman came closer. Her hair was in tangles, covered in soot, and her dress had small holes singed throughout, though leaving her covered in the right places.

Clearly, she'd been on *The Sapphire*, but something in her eyes said that she'd survived alone. "I remember you, Monsieur, from the lifeboats. You caught us before we could fall..."

"I...yes..." Erik's fingers subtly clenched, as if subconsciously remembering grabbing hold of the chains.

"You...must forgive me for not thanking you sooner..." The woman lowered her gaze in a way that made my heart ache for her, a stranger, right then and there.

"It was a traumatizing night for all of us...There's nothing to forgive..." I offered a smile, motioning for her to sit with us. As she did, I continued. "I'm Sarah Dupree, and this is my husband, Erik."

"Helaine..." At the single word, something broke inside of her. Thankfully Erik was right there; she surely would have fallen to the ground had he not gently directed her head to his shoulder. He'd gotten so used to the silent act of comfort, raising two daughters and of course being married to someone as emotional as myself.

Between bouts of sobs, Helaine told us how she'd been named for her aunt, who'd taken her in as a toddler after her parents' passing. She'd then become a hired companion to her godmother, her aunt's best friend, three years prior, when a sudden illness took her namesake away. "We...were going to America...to get a change of scenery...give me a fresh start somewhere..." Helaine explained shakily. "Th–the explosion woke me...a–and I went to check on her...She...the flames...I–it was too late..." She whimpered into the offered handkerchief. "B–but I could just hear her...I felt something telling me to save myself...to...carry on their legacy..."

"Oh my dear..." I touched her shoulder then. "What a burden you've been carrying..."

"I've no choice...It's mine to carry...There's no one else..."

"I was the same way, for the longest time..." Erik's voice was raspy as he fought back the old hurts. Slowly, he told his story and how he'd come to know the love and comfort of God's presence. "All those years of loneliness, and He was right there, waiting for me to open the door and let Him in..."

"I...D–do you suppose He's waiting for me, too?" At her question, I couldn't help but smile to myself and thank God silently for placing us right there in that precise moment to be His voice and His arms. As we each spoke our 'amens', Helaine lifted her head, her face glowing with newfound peace that could only come from above.

"Helaine, how would you like to remain with us? At least until we get to America..."

"Are you sure?"

"Of course! In fact, we insist..." Erik smiled determinedly. Even Helaine knew that, with a look like that, there'd be no use arguing. "Now, shall we head down to the inn for breakfast?" The owners, as I'd been told, had been gracious enough to allow most of the survivors to board there as we awaited the next ship, meals included. The doctor and his wife had fed Erik and I up til now, and so we'd be experiencing the inn's hospitality for the first time together.

"We shall!" I grinned, and at the sight of Helaine's eyes lighting up, I could tell she'd only just now regained her appetite.

****

A warm breeze set the curtain of weeping willow branches dancing, the roar of a distant waterfall blocking out any audible cue that the wind was blowing. *Erik was right once again...I* smiled to myself as he stopped my wheelchair by the brook. We'd invited Helaine to join us for lunch, and the two of them busied themselves with setting up the picnic beneath the willow. Judging from this spot alone, one would never guess they were on an island. It was as if we'd passed into a whole other world. "I'm sorry we could not save your camera or writings..." Erik handed me a plate, seeming to read my thoughts before I could piece them together myself.

"That's quite alright..." I touched his arm. "It is a beautiful place, but I certainly won't forget it before I can describe it on paper..."

"Even so, I'll try to get us both some materials so that we can capture it properly in our own ways while we're here..." As we began eating, I looked over to ask Helaine if she wanted to sit closer. My words were halted when I saw that she had curled up on the blanket, her food untouched. Following my gaze, Erik sighed. "She hasn't slept...not since that night. I could see it in her eyes right away...She's just been wandering the island aimlessly..."

"Oh, Erik..." My heart sank. "How can we possibly leave her to fend for herself in America?"

"We won't." He brought his fingers up to my face, caressing as he gently brushed at the first of my tears. "We'll stay with her until she's found her footing." I leaned into his touch, taking comfort in knowing he shared my concerns as our parenting instincts took over. Once he saw that I was at peace again, he took one of the blankets from around me and carefully draped it over our companion. "Will you be alright to stay with her while I see to some things at the inn?"

"Of course..." I smiled, knowing he was about to work his magic. After we shared a kiss, I watched him go before I settled more comfortably in my chair.

Between the gentle breeze and the music of nearby birds lulling me in and out of sleep, I did not know how long he was gone. Helaine continued dozing, but I was perfectly content in the peace and quiet of our surroundings. I was only brought back to full alertness when the willow branches parted, revealing Erik's return with the innkeeper. "He'll be showing us to a room on the ground level of the inn..." Erik explained as the innkeeper carefully lifted Helaine into his arms. "I promised a couple nights of entertaining the others at the piano in return, and I've exchanged a few commissions for some dresses for the two of you, and the paper and ink of course..."

"You really are too much for words, Erik!" I grasped his hand as he moved to stand behind my chair.

"Nonsense!" He scoffed playfully. "They're practical needs, and I have the time."

"Still...it's yet another reminder of one of the many things I love about you..."

"Well it's all thanks to *you*, my dear, for letting God use you to shine light and hope into my life and give me plentiful reasons to share what I have with others."

We arrived at our room in no time, and once Erik saw to Helaine's comforts, he hung a curtain up between the two beds. Thanking the innkeeper, he then helped me into the larger bed, sitting behind me so that he could gently run a brush through my hair. The soothing act was enough to lull me back to sleep, and I suspected he'd planned it that way. His words as he switched to braiding my locks proved that I was correct. "I'll help you change once you've rested...I put you through quite a bit of excitement today..." He left a trail of kisses down the side of my neck, slowly wrapping his arms around me.

"I don't regret a moment of it..." I smiled more, leaning back against him. "You're so good to me..."

"And you me..." He rested his lips on top of my head, tenderly massaging my shoulders until we both drifted off to sleep.

****

####*THREE*****

    By the time we set sail for America once again, my arm and face had healed enough for the stitches and remaining bandages to be removed. It was advised, however, that I remain in the wheelchair until our return to France. Helaine's strength had also returned, and she proved herself to be a wonderful companion and gifted caregiver if ever Erik's fulfillments of promises took him from my side when I needed help. It was as if I had taken the place of her employer in her godmother's absence, although she refused to accept even a promise of future payment. She insisted that simply allowing her to remain with us was sufficient. Still, Erik and I both silently dreamed up ways we could eventually repay her.

    As New York finally drifted into view, I had to blink several times in order to see the reality of color rather than in the black and white of photographs I'd glimpsed so often before. It looked far different from when I had visited it in my time, and yet so many other things were the same. For once I was thankful to be confined to the wheelchair; otherwise I would have surely been caught up in the bustle, carried away from Erik's steadying arm. The three of us waited until the rest of the passengers disembarked, following them through the process of ensuring our freedom to travel through my homeland. Thankfully, Erik had done his research well to make sure there were no questions or doubts of my origins. We had a daughter to see, and we'd been delayed enough.

    As we maneuvered our way onto the ferry that would take us from Ellis Island to the main city, one of the uniformed men hesitated in his rehearsed greeting. "Mother! Father! Whatever happened to you?"

"Samuel!" I burst into tears of excitement and relief that I hadn't realized I was holding back.

"Janelle's been worried sick! She's only been able to continue singing because I promised I'd keep my eyes peeled with every ferry of passengers..."

Erik explained our ordeal and introduced Helaine to our son-in-law over the time it took to reach the docks. Escorting us off, Samuel stuffed a handful of bills into Erik's hand. "There will be carriages waiting. Have one bring you to the Metropolitan Opera House, at the corner of Broadway and Thirty-Ninth. Janelle will want to see you right away...Never mind that she's in rehearsal."

"The feeling's more than mutual!" I assured him as we parted ways. During the carriage ride to the Opera House, I was struck by the absence of car horns and the hissing and squeaking brakes of buses and trucks. To be sure, I had been in this time long enough that such traffic would have shocked me completely, but it was so odd to see such familiarity without it. At least there were the subways and elevated trains to bring some sort of compromise of normalcy as I watched Erik and Helaine take it all in. There was so much I wanted to show them or see for myself for the first time, but I had to wait to make sure those places already were in existence. It was a discussion that I would have to have with Erik when we were again alone.

For the time being, I was just happy to see the old Metropolitan Opera House, which would be torn down and replaced by an office tower by the time I was born. The yellow brick exterior stood out much more than the size and shape; one never would have known that a fire had gutted the building over ten years prior, but Erik and I had Janelle's letter to prove it. She also wrote us that the interior had been redesigned two years before our arrival now, and Erik and I were both eager to see it for ourselves.

    Sure enough, as we entered, if it weren't for the sound of our daughter's voice rehearsing, we would have certainly forgotten our purpose here. Awestruck silence washed over us as we made our way past the rows of house seats toward the stage. So lost was she in the character she was portraying that only when they took a break did she notice our presence. "Mama! Papa!" She squealed just like her birth mother, but her joy of seeing us wasn't in the least bit over-dramatic. Within seconds, she was weeping in the middle of our arms, her tears of pure relief that we were alive. Even I got caught up in the moment, rising from my wheelchair with all my weight on my good leg. Only after her initial wave of tearful elation subsided did she step back and take notice of the changes to my appearance. Seeing the questions forming on her lips, I shook my head.

    "We'll fill you in later...Right now we won't keep you from your rehearsal..."

    "Of course..." her smile returned as she reluctantly went back to the stage, and Erik helped me back into my chair.

****

    Rehearsals ended close enough to suppertime that we opted to make our explanations and introductions at a table outside one of the restaurants in Times Square. The street was so busy that barely anyone bothered to look our way, allowing us to focus entirely on catching Janelle up on everything we'd lived through. She greeted Helaine warmly, insisting the girl not hesitate to request anything of her that she might need. At this, Erik beamed proudly at the woman Janelle had become. Just then, a scrawny, dirt-caked hand reached out from behind him, snatching the roll off his plate. In true Phantom form and instinct, Erik wasted no time in whirling around to catch the thief, grasping the wrist firmly enough that the bread was instantly dropped onto his lap. His face quickly softened, however, when his eyes fell on the crutch barely holding up the boy's trembling figure. "I–I'm sorry, sir...I let my hunger get the best of me..."

"How old are you, boy? Shouldn't you be home with your family at this hour?"

"I haven't got one. Folks died a few years back. Tried my hand at being a newsie, but people grew numb to my limp...thought it was an act I overdid to win their pity..."

"Pity's not what you really want, boy..." Erik shook his head, releasing the child's hand before pulling out an empty chair for him. "Pity may get you a moment's sympathy...a single coin...a crust of bread...and then they move on, having done their good deed for the day, leaving you to fend for yourself the rest of the time." As he relayed his wisdom, he motioned to the waiter.

In between gulps of the meal Erik had ordered for him, the boy explained that his name was Ethan, aged nine years old. His leg had been broken when he was only two, but because his parents couldn't afford a doctor, it never mended properly. "The others said the limp's all I've got to my advantage...I couldn't cover all the miles they do in a day, and if people stop believing me, what can I do?" Ethan shrugged dejectedly, finishing off his entire glass of milk all at once.

"You tell me..." Erik raised an eyebrow. "There must be something you like to do...that you're really good at..."

"I liked going to school...Did real well, until I had to stop so's I could make a living. I even helped the younger kids...helped me block out the others' laughing at me..."

"Then you must return to it...Perhaps you're meant to teach...You cannot do that living on the streets, stealing from others..."

"But I have no choice!" Ethan's eyes filled with frustrated tears. "I gotta support myself...I got no one to look after me...No one'll hire a cripple..."

"You're wrong..." Janelle's soft voice broke in. "Come with us tonight, to my home. I'm sure my husband will take very little convincing..." The compassion and understanding in her eyes brought tears to mine; after all these years, she remembered what it was like to be taken under someone else's wing in her own mother's absence.

"Y–you mean it? Really?" Ethan sniffled, almost afraid to even hope.

"Every word...You're all of nine years old, Ethan...Now is your time to be a child. Save your worries for much later on..."

About an hour later, we arrived at Janelle's house right at the same time as Samuel. Although surprised to see the now sleeping boy seated next to his wife in the carriage, he did not hesitate to carry Ethan inside. While the exterior differed little from the surrounding townhouses, we were taken aback by the interior's reflection of Janelle's success on stage. "I'll have the library set up as a guest room for you immediately..." Janelle assured us. "You'll find it quite comfortable. The children will already be in bed, but I imagine you need your rest."

"Thank you, my dear..." I smiled gratefully as she led Helaine upstairs behind Samuel and Ethan. She returned moments later, keeping us company as we waited for our room.

"I want to thank you, Papa, for tonight..." She loosely hugged Erik around the neck, sincerity locked on her face. "Living here, in the city, we learn early on to keep our guard up, mind our own business...it's a necessary cruelty...there are plenty of dishonest people...teaching children to be dishonest as well...survive at all costs...I forgot that the innocents are out there too...And you taught me something tonight as you were teaching him something else entirely..."

"It's not very different at all, Janelle..." Erik kissed her head tenderly. "You both needed to hope for the good..." At that, he glanced in my direction. "As did I, so very long ago..."

"It's true for all of us, sooner or later..." I spoke up around the lump in my throat, through the curtain of exhaustion. "It's up to those who find it to pass it on...To hope is to live..."

Finally, the maid appeared to signal that her work was done, and Janelle thanked her profusely for staying up, granting her the following day off with pay. Our good nights exchanged, I surrendered to sleep before Erik could even lift me out of the chair into the makeshift bed.

****

"**No.**" Erik shoved his chair back and stood, abandoning his barely-touched noon meal. "Absolutely not!" As he stormed out, I made a clumsy attempt to wheel myself after him, throwing an apologetic roll of my eyes over my shoulder to Janelle.

"Erik, you're not being fair!" I huffed, nearly toppling over as we rounded a corner in the hallway.

"I won't be talked into it!" He whirled around, and I took the opportunity to roll past him and block the entrance to our room.

"I don't see why you're taking her side anyway! You know the trouble she caused me!"

"Of course I know!" I took his hand, giving it a gentle squeeze. "But I also know *you*, Erik...The man I married is full of love, if not for her then for the daughter we share with her...he wants nothing more than to see her and our grandchildren grow following the best example possible. And I know how much this would mean for Janelle. Surely you can't deny her this..." Watching his face, I could see the stubbornness melting away, though he still refused to meet my gaze. "Besides, the torment from then wasn't entirely one-sided, my love...So for her to request to speak with you again...it must be important..."

"It appears to be important to everyone but me..." Erik heaved a grunted sigh, glaring past me out the library's bay window.

"Need I remind you once again that the world's not against you?" I used my thumb to caress the back of his knuckles, coaxing him to finally look my way.

"You *are* my world..." He sighed again, sounding less defeated, more exhausted. "You and the children..." He covered my hand with his, looking down at the floor. "It was just...so much easier sharing Janelle with her when the distance between us was so great...Even when I planned this trip, seeing Carlotta never entered my mind, knowing she's bedridden..."

"I know, my love..." I offered a small smile, bringing his hand up so I could rest my cheek against it. "And the sooner we humor her, the sooner we can return to enjoying our time here."

"It seems that I underestimated your ability to change my mind..." His lips finally turned up into a tight smile. "How quickly I forget your countless victories in the past..."

"It's not a contest, love...Nor a battle..." I grinned. "But I would accept a prize of you wheeling me back to the dining room. For some reason I have more of an appetite than before..." I threw him a teasing pout, rubbing my sore arms.

"Well, good, because for some reason I've lost mine, and so you may have my helping." He let out a half-bitter chuckle, proceeding to wheel me in the direction of our food.

"Do try, Erik...for Janelle's sake..." I looked back at him, and he stopped the chair long enough to plant a kiss.

"For Janelle's sake...and yours...and mine because I just know I won't hear the end of it otherwise..."

"I believe you're finally getting it!" I giggled, returning the kiss with a smirk.

****

"Come in..." The voice that called from the other side of the door was unrecognizable, save for the thick Italian accent. Erik and I exchanged a look of confused shock before entering Carlotta's room. The wall-to-wall pink decor eased our minds immediately that it was indeed her that had spoken, and yet the form on the bed made its best attempt to contradict such assurance. Her skin was pale and wrinkled, not a trace of makeup to be found. Her graying curls draped around her face in an absolute mess. She looked at us with a total lack of fierceness, not a single demand readying itself on her lips. I was grateful to already be sitting down; Erik had to fumble for the nearest chair to collapse into. All his fight and stubbornness had completely dissipated. "My, it's as if the Phantom has seen a ghost..." The tiniest spark of a smile broke through the tense silence, and all at once we both remembered how to breathe.

"What...have you done to yourself...?" Erik blurted, unapologetic out of sheer candidness.

"You should know. You knew back then I should have stopped while I was on top. I let this sickness take the stage out from under me. My singing voice has been gone ever since." She looked away, reaching for a glass of water. "It's just as well...I could not have gone through another fire at another opera house..." Tears trickled down her face then; we could see that this time, they were real; in fact, they ran as though they were always present, not at all dependent on whether or not she acknowledged them. "I loved him, Monsieur...my Piangi...you took him from me...and I need to know why..." When she looked our way again, she seemed to have aged all the more. "Did you really hate me that much?" At this, Erik let out his breath slowly, as if he'd been waiting for that very question to be asked of him.

"No, Senora...As I said before, contrary to what you may believe, I never, ever, meant to truly hurt you. If I had, I would have right from the start. I told you, his death had nothing to do with you..."

"What did he ever do to you that was far worse than anything I did?" She dabbed at her eyes, her first admission of her part in the animosity.

"Nothing..." Erik shook his head, staring down at his hands. "It was the way he treated Betzazel...the dwarf that mimicked him..."

"I...don't understand..." Carlotta blinked, genuinely ignorant of any issue.

"No, you wouldn't, would you?" Erik lifted his head, his old anger rising up. "He was good enough to be up on stage with your Piangi, but once the curtain closed, not once was he allowed to socialize with *your* crowd. He was like a child's toy that got put in a box when Piangi was done with him...An extension of his costumes...a mask...his only purpose being to entertain..." His anger now took the form of tears that silenced the both of us listening; this was something he'd kept bottled up even from me. "You didn't see...Piangi especially should have...how much he looked up to him as a brother...how he was gifted in other areas...He made so many dolls and toys for the little ones when they were sad or scared...made them laugh again with his wordless antics..."

"But...he was always chasing after the skirts..." Carlotta feebly pointed.

"Not one of us is perfect, Señora. We all have our faults...No, that's just an excuse. Perhaps if Piangi had taken the time to give him the attention he longed for, he never would have felt the need to go looking for it elsewhere..."

"Still, you haven't said a single thing that rightfully condemns a man to death!"

"You're right." His quick agreement shocked even her tears to stillness. "I was looking at the issue as a man who could have easily been right there with Betzazel...because I *was*, as a child. I was put on display for however long the crowds would look, and then I was locked away...hidden...neglected...It was those old feelings that drove me to actions...actions I now, as I have for some time, regret." Silence fell on us all then, as we processed everything. After several moments, Erik stood, readying to leave. "I do not seek, nor expect, your forgiveness, Carlotta. I have made peace with God, and that's all that matters. I only thank you for not using all this time and distance to turn Janelle or the children against me."

"It's not like I didn't try..." she scoffed, finally showing signs of her old self. "But every time I did, I was reminded that you, too, had the same opportunity...but whenever you saw need to correct her, you never once mentioned my name as a bad example...and when Janelle told me how you broke the news to her about being adopted, you still did not shame me..."

"That was all Sarah..." Erik pointed. "Had it not been for her, I would have carried Janelle off for fear of her encountering you..." His words caused her to seemingly notice my presence for the very first time. If she was taken aback by my appearance, her gratitude did not allow it to show.

"Thank you...for keeping my daughter from making the same mistakes as me..." She then retreated back into her shell of sadness, her silence indicating the visit to be over. Erik placed his hand on my chair, but I wheeled it forward, out of his grasp.

"You speak as though your life is over...as if time has run out...But you're wrong. Janelle still thinks the world of you, Carlotta...You've done so much for her and her children...more than you give yourself credit for...It's not too late to be with them...enjoy life with them, making memories...You are not a failure."

"But what can I do? I cannot sing...I cannot leave this bed..."

"Let them visit you then...They're more than your devotees. They're your family. I'm sure Lydia would love to bring her dolls so you can help her dress them up..."

"Her mother can do that..." She waved off the suggestion.

"There's still so much that they can learn only from you..." I gently touched her arm. "Mistakes are made to be learned from and passed on so that others don't walk the same path. Tell them your story...your love for Piangi...perhaps then they will learn how to treat others who are different..."

"Si..." she finally let a small smile appear. "Perhaps my beloved can still make things right..." She then looked over to

Erik, who was hovering by the door. "Betzazel...what happened to him?"

"I'll surely ask around, once we return to France..."

"Please do...I wish to apologize, if I can..."

"I'm certain he'd appreciate it..." Erik offered a tight smile, still processing the entire conversation.

We exchanged goodbyes shortly after, and then Erik and I opted to spend some time exploring Central Park. We discussed nothing aside from present observances as they came our way. At one point, he plopped down on a bench, and I maneuvered myself carefully out of my chair so I could sit beside him. As soon as our hands touched, his dam burst as his head collapsed onto my shoulder. I held his shaking form for several moments in complete silence, soothingly rubbing his back and shoulders. "That...was the hardest thing I've ever done...Even compared to socializing with Christine and Raoul..."

"I'm so proud of you, my love..." I gently kissed at his tears.

"I...was just so tired of the bitter taste...I thought I hid it well enough, but whenever she came up in conversation with Janelle, I could see the pain it was still causing without me saying a word..."

"Well now we can all start with a fresh page..."

"Yes..." he nodded as another wave of tears spilled out. "I owe Janelle a dinner for starters...open conversation to clear the air..."

"She'll love that..." I grinned, lightly kissing him. "Right now I think you could do with some music...Perhaps the opera house has a violin you can borrow..."

"You know me so well, my dear..." He tenderly returned the kiss, his tears finally drying.

"Well, I knew it was either that or a brownie..." I teased, smoothing his collar.

"We'll stop at a bakery on the way." He vowed with a chuckle. Although our plans were set, we lingered on the bench for close to another hour, just enjoying being wrapped in each others' embrace surrounded by the music of songbirds in the trees above us.

****

####*FOUR*####

As previously planned, we spent a month in the city. I was more than willing to allow Janelle and Samuel to suggest attractions and sites that we simply had to visit and explore; I was so fearful I would let something slip otherwise. Between sightseeing ventures and attending performances at other theaters as well as at the Met, we helped Helaine keep watch for any employment opportunities she might be comfortable with. Our search was fruitless, however. She was far too personable for factory or cleaning work, yet underqualified on paper for any other possibility. She was of course open to the idea of college, but insistent on paying her own way.

One evening, the solution hit me so hard that the book I'd been barely reading fell to my lap. "Of course..!!" Erik looked over, eyebrow raised as he lifted the volume to note the title.

"My dear, you sound as though you've solved a mystery...but this is '*Black Beauty*', and you said you're already familiar with the tale..."

"Hmm? Oh...no...that wasn't it..." I rolled my eyes at myself, setting the book aside. "It's Helaine...I don't know why I didn't think of it before..." I shifted my position so I was facing him fully. "What if she were to come back to France with us? Neither of us are getting any younger, and she took such good care of me on the boat..."

"Did she not come here for a fresh start, though? A change of scenery?"

"That is true..." I admitted. "But I see no harm in running the idea past her...see what she thinks..." He studied me for a few minutes then, smiling softly.

"You've come to think of her as another daughter, haven't you?"

"How can I not?" I returned the smile, taking his hand. "What we went through...our shared ordeal...how we prayed with her...it makes us like family..."

"You're thinking about Antoin, too, aren't you? Always the romantic writer..." He chuckled, tickling my neck playfully.

"I can't keep anything from the Phantom, can I?" I giggled, relenting.

"Never." He whispered, covering my lips with his. "But it is amusing watching you try..."

"I don't hear you dismissing the notion..." I pointed, smirking.

"Well *I've* learned to not even try to argue with you..."

"Only took twenty-six years..." I teased, scooting closer so I could lean back against him.

"Twenty-six years..." He set his own book aside so that he could wrap his arms around me. "And our love has only grown deeper and stronger, even with all the reasons I've given you to give up on me..."

"I could never!" I poked his ribs. "Sometimes I think you only talk like that to get me fired up!" My accusation was met with a smirk that always caused butterflies to form in my stomach.

"You're finally getting it..." He gently kissed along my scars to my lips. "Perhaps there's more Phantom to *you* than you realize...It would seem as though I've had an effect on you..."

"Well *that's* an understatement!" I returned the kiss through my giggle, reaching up to take his hand. "Quite the effect on me indeed...even before we met..."

"Love as true as ours...time and space mean nothing..." He gently brushed his fingers through my hair. "I can see why you want Helaine and Antoin to experience that as well. If it's meant to be, nothing can stop it. Even if it's not, I see no harm in an introduction. We'll pray for wisdom for all of us...Unblinded eyes so we don't miss what God is trying to show us and teach us..."

"And courage to accept whatever His plan is, and move with it..."

"Of course..." He nodded. "Stubborn as we tend to be..." I could hear in his tone that he was speaking more of himself, and I frowned, giving his hand a gentle squeeze.

"My love, you're only proving your own point. You must forgive yourself...His timing has been perfect with everything the both of us have been through to bring us to this moment, right here, right now. And it will continue to be perfect to bring us through to eternity..."

"I am trying, Sarah, I really am..." He carefully pulled me closer into a tighter embrace. "My biggest regret still haunts me though...Every morning, waking up beside you...How much precious time and wonderful memories were lost because I refused to admit my feelings for you to myself for so long..."

"You're right in that we can't get that time back, my love..." I turned to face him again, releasing his hand so I could brush my fingers against his face. "We can make up for it though, by not wasting the time we do have in the present by focusing solely on the past..."

"You're right again, Madame Dupree..." He finally allowed the smirk to return, kissing my fingers as he put out the lamp. "You're absolutely right..."

****

A few days later, we were on a train bound for Plymouth, New Hampshire. We chose to not bring up the idea of returning to France to Helaine, as Janelle offered to continue helping her with her search in our absence. Thankfully, they were all satisfied with the explanation that we were simply going to see the place I grew up in, and that we'd only be gone for a couple of weeks. Samuel and Janelle even gifted us a generous sum to "really spoil" ourselves and enjoy some alone time together. As Erik tucked it into his pocket, I just knew he was already plotting something from the sparkle dancing in his eye. I chose to say nothing and allow him to have his fun; I could tell that he still had some recovering to do from the conversation with Carlotta. Even with all the time that had passed between that day and this one, with the occasional full family visit, he remained quiet and distant in her company. Never cold or impolite, but certainly withdrawn unless the focus was on Janelle or the children.

I took his hand as we settled into our seat on the train, and he responded with a knowing smile. "Excited to see how much has changed?"

"Very..." I nodded. "And how much is the same..." He fell silent then, watching me and seemingly deep in thought.

"I feel that I must warn you, my dear. The place, even the structure might be the same. But it's the people who would have made it feel like home. As excluded as I was from the goings on of the Opera House, there's a reason why I chose to use the rose trinket...the same reason I could not stay angry with you for choosing to join me there. The silence would have added weight to the chains of loneliness...I never would have survived...Not without them making music...not without you keeping me company...That's what made it a home..." Before I realized they were falling, he brushed away my tears with his thumb. "Oh, my dear, I didn't mean..." He gently pulled me closer so I could bury my face against his chest. "You gave up so much when you made your choice...so that I could know what it's like to have a loving family...It's a sacrifice I've not acknowledged nearly enough, and yet it was your greatest one..."

"I...still don't regret it..." I managed between sniffles.

"Yes, you do. Just a little bit..." He lifted my chin so I could see his comforting smile. "You regret that they could not share in our life together...that I and the children will never know them. Don't you start being stubborn, Sarah. Don't deny your love for them. It's alright to miss them. It doesn't mean your love for me is any smaller. It only means just how large your heart truly is..."

"I...do regret that..." I slowly nodded as fresh tears spilled out. "They would have loved you..."

"And even though I never met them, my dear, I know that they would be proud of the woman you've become. I know *I* am..."

"And I'm proud of you, Erik..." I rested my head on his shoulder, closing my eyes as I allowed the rest of my tears to flow. He spoke no more, caressing my face in a steady rhythm until I dozed off.

It was just as well that I slept through most of the train ride; as emotional a state I was already in, the last thing I needed would have been to add bitterness to the mix, not having my small digital camera. Even if I had my current one, it would be useless to attempt capturing the scenery whipping by the windows. I think Erik must have sensed this, which was why he was so quick to lull me to sleep. What neither of us factored in was how the long rocking motion would affect my stomach. Thankfully, the hour was late enough and the train station close enough to the

Pemigewasset House that it was no time before I was settled into the large cozy bed. "I've ordered a cup of tea with toast and jam with my supper, should you feel up to trying..." Erik sat behind me, tenderly undoing what was left of my braid before brushing out the tangles.

"Thank you, love..." I managed just above a whisper, doubtful I'd still be awake when it arrived.

"Shall I unpack your nightgown?" He kissed my head, setting the brush aside.

"Please..." I nodded, knowing I needn't tell him I'd need help changing. Instead, he went above and beyond my unspoken request, gently running a cool damp cloth over my back and shoulders before slipping the nightgown over my head. "You're so wonderful to me..." I smiled weakly up at him as I finally lowered myself to the pillow.

"Hush now, my dear...Get your rest..." He returned the smile, stilling my lips from any further conversation with a kiss. Dipping the cloth into the water once more, he pressed it to my forehead. "Shall I sing to you?"

"You know I'll always say yes to that..." I grinned, my eyes closed under the comforting pressure of the cloth. Gathering me in his arms, he obliged long enough for his music to drift through the background of my dreams.

****

By the time I awoke around noon the following day, my stomach and head felt mostly back to normal. Carefully sitting up, I noticed Erik's side of the bed was unslept in; he was instead sitting at the desk by the window, his back to me as he hunched over a sketch book. The sight sent my mind back to the scene from the movie when Christine woke up in his lair. From there, my mind drifted slightly forward to a memory I had never addressed to him because it had felt so entangled in my dreams that I had tucked the thought away for all the time in between. I remained silent though, letting him work. My leg still lacked the strength to allow me to approach from behind and greet him with an embrace while sneaking a peek at whatever he was working on, just as I had done so many times before. Instead, I relished the ability to lazily admire the artist I loved from afar; even with his back to me, I could imagine the focused expression on his face as he moved his pen across the paper with such care and ability.

Several minutes passed before he finally stretched, putting the pen aside as he turned to check on me. "You're awake..!" He grinned, crossing the room to sit beside me.

"Have you not slept?" I reached for his hand.

"Inspiration hit..." He shook his head, kissing my fingers before caressing my face with the back of his hand. "How are you feeling?"

"Better...a little hungry..."

"That's good...you fell asleep almost immediately...barely moved all night..."

"It was that voice of yours that did it." I pointed, once again reminded of that unburied memory. "Erik...?" I sat up further. "When...we were in the caverns and you were still not speaking to me...I...seem to recall one restless night when I was dreaming about my family...I...suddenly heard a voice...as quiet and gentle as a breeze, singing to me...comforting me...All this time, I thought it was merely part of my dream. But, last night, the same effect came over me...It was you back then, wasn't it...?" He hesitated before answering, closing his eyes against the rising emotions apparent in his face.

"I remember that night. I could not ignore your tears, despite my anger, despite my vow of silence...So many nights, I cried those same tears, except yours were over that which you lost. Mine were over that which I never had. Both the very same thing...I knew what would help...I could not keep it to myself..."

"Oh, Erik...You really did care, even back then..."

"Even back then..." he echoed slowly, his eyes watering. "I think that was when I first noticed my feelings for you...and I was angry with myself for them...Angry with you for causing them just by existing...I was clinging so hard still to my dreams about Christine...A love I thought so wrongly was real..."

"And yet you still went through with comforting me..." I reminded him, gently brushing away his tears. "You fought your own stubbornness, even though you weren't ready to face the reason why. That's one of the deepest, strongest forms of love there is..."

"It's the same love you showed me, right from the start. Even though you were more ready to embrace it, you waited for me..."

"I have my own confession, Erik...I heard your tears as well back then." At that, he shook his head.

"They'd become so intertwined in my existence in those surroundings, I grew numb to them. Never knowing if they were part of my nightmares or if they were actually audible...I'm afraid I don't know how I would have reacted to you coming to my aid in comfort...I fear I honestly might have hurt you if you had indeed startled me out of my sleep, restless as it was..."

"I still wanted to, my love. Every part of me longed to forget the agreement and hold you in my arms. The only thing that held me back was the thought of upsetting you further...I wasn't afraid of what you might do to me. I just felt God reminding me that you just weren't ready for that yet. Now, I realize we were both showing love while thinking we were keeping it hidden, just in the very act of fighting it..." I giggled slightly at the irony. "I'd call us foolish and silly for it, but I'm reminded of a saying I had on my wall back home: 'If you love something, let it go. If it leaves, it was never yours. If it returns, love it forever.'"

"I certainly could have used that bit of wisdom long ago..." Erik shook his head with a chuckle. "Not that I'd have listened...No, we both needed to learn it for ourselves...live it...feel it..." He ran the back of his fingers down my cheek. "And my dear, I'm so glad you were meant to be mine..."

Tender expressions of fresh gratitude soon replaced any lingering thoughts of regret, and as I watched him sleep after our wordless conversation ended, I knew there would be no exploring my hometown's history until the next day. The rumble in my stomach, however, threatened to steal my joy as I stubbornly snuggled further against him. How I longed just in this moment, for the convenience of a cell phone to order us food with! Of course, there was a telephone in the room(the old-but-new technology of which Erik and I both had to learn), but it was situated on a little table between two arm chairs, frustratingly out of reach. My heart pleaded with me to stay beside my husband, my stomach beckoning me from our bed, but my body spoke to my head about its limits. Thus, the three forces battled each other until my stomach's noises became too much to bear. Ever so careful to not disturb Erik's much-needed slumber, I eased my legs over the edge of the bed. *Progress.* I needed only for something to hold onto. Looking around, I figured out a theoretic plan of action, provided my good leg held out. Nodding to myself, I slowly stood, gripping the edges of the nightstand. I stayed there for several moments, letting my body adjust before I reached for the closet doorknob. From there, I took hold of the large planter for support before finally lunging carefully at one of the arm chairs. Breathless, I reached for the telephone, letting my exhaustion subside before I managed to mumble off two orders of chicken a la king and fudge brownies. Replacing the receiver, I glanced warily back at the bed, wondering if I had the strength to return. *No, better to rest here for a bit, lest I collapse right on top of Erik and wake him,* I decided, but exasperatedly pointed to myself that I should fetch my robe and clean myself up a bit before the food was to arrive. Rolling my eyes, I pulled myself back up, inching my way along the walls and every steady bit of furnishings before finally reaching the bathroom.

By the time I'd freshened up, gulped down some water, and thrown my robe on over my nightgown, I was feeling much more energized. Now that I'd put my good leg to work and gotten the hang of moving around, I wasn't quite ready to crawl back into bed. Instead, I put my mind to sitting at the desk and going over everything I'd written out for my family to find. Only when I lowered myself to the chair and saw Erik's sketch book did I remember he'd been working on it all night.

It was open to an unfinished family portrait, as recent as we could all look before *The Sapphire* went down. Overtaken by curiosity, I flipped back to the previous drawings—solo portraits of each child and grandchild, a visual of us watching our children take their first steps or say their prayers, one of Janelle's first performance as we looked on with pride, and even an imagined wedding portrait of the two of us. "Oh, Erik..." I whispered around the lump in my throat.

"I got to thinking about what we said...about your family not being able to be a part of our life..." He wrapped his arms around me from behind, but I was too emotional to be startled. Instead, I leaned against him, resting my head on his arm. He carefully moved so that he was kneeling beside me, never letting go as he handed me a handkerchief. "I figured out a way for them to at least see the most important parts..."

"Erik, it's absolutely perfect! I didn't even think to ask you..."

"Nor did you have to, my dear..." He softly brushed at my tears with his lips. "What I *do* want to know is how you even remotely managed to get all the way over here..."

"I...didn't want to wake you..." I threw him a sheepish grin before explaining my hunger and method. At that, he stifled a chuckle before slowly going over to the closet door and opening it to reveal my wheelchair.

"W—why yo—!!!" I sputtered, on the verge of exhausted hysteria as I flung the crumpled handkerchief at him.

"I'm so sorry..." He laughed, failing miserably in his attempt to be sympathetic. "In my defense, I didn't think you'd actually try!" Putting his open palms up in front of himself protectively, he cautiously made his way back to me. To my dismay, as I looked around I found nothing to grab to even jokingly threaten to throw. Instead, I chose a half-hearted, over-dramatic pout, crossing my arms. "Now, my dear, think of it this way...Had you known you needed only to open that door, you never would have pushed yourself to seeing just how strong you really are..." By then, he was at my side again, the truth of his words sinking in and softening me up.

"I suppose..." I sighed, unwilling to completely give up the play-fight. "...I suppose if you give me half your brownie when it comes, we can call it even!" At that, he gasped, playing along with my dramatics.

"Never!" He then grabbed my hands, lifting my fingers to his lips as he knelt down. "Would you settle for a massage after we eat?"

"...That's a low blow when I'm this exhausted, and you know it!" I yanked my hands back, then threw him a grin as I caressed his face. "...but I accept!"

✳✳

####*SIX*####

The next morning, Erik rented us a carriage so that we could explore without explaining to anyone our reason for visiting my family's future home. As I directed him up the hill, my mixed emotions threatened to once again affect my stomach and nerves; it was a wonder how I was able to take in even my small breakfast of toast, jam, and coffee. I clutched the wrapped parcel containing his drawings and my writings tighter to my chest, finally getting my eyes on the property. The house itself was still under construction, which brought a sense of relief to our plan. The walls were already in place, as well as the stairs and all three stories of floors. The roof and siding would be next, then the drywall. Thankfully, it was early enough that the workers still had yet to arrive, but it would be best to move quickly. "Do you know yet where it should go?" Erik placed his hand on mine, motioning to the parcel.

"The top of the stairs...halfway down the left-side wall. In my time, the drywall will start to fall apart, exposing the lath layer underneath."

"Would you like to try to come with me?" I hesitated for a moment, tears of frustration ready to fall. I had so been looking forward to walking through the building that would one day hold so many countless memories for me that I longed to share with him while we were actually there.

"I would only slow you down..." I shook my head instead, managing a small smile of reassurance. Although I could tell he saw through my obvious mask, he chose to not pursue the subject. Instead, he placed a gentle, comforting kiss on my trembling lower lip, caressing my face with the back of his hand.

"I'll draw you a picture later...in full detail..." He slowly took the package from me and climbed down. "Don't go wandering now..." He attempted to lighten my mood, jokingly reminding me of the day before.

"Only my mind will..." I smiled more, hoping my face reflected my gratitude.

"Good girl..." He chuckled lightly, giving my hand one more squeeze before he disappeared into the structure. In the time he was gone, I did indeed let my thoughts wander, skipping over the cherished memories to envision my family in the future, uncovering the package. They would first see my letter, reading through my words of love and assurance before coming to an almost novelized explanation of Erik's and my story. Next, they'd find his drawings, each one captioned, until they reached his final contribution: a letter he would not let me read, but he described as an introduction filled with promises to care for me. The package itself was labeled as a time capsule to be opened in a hundred and thirteen years; I figured that the odd number would provide ample time for my future self to be gone before its presence was noticed. I could picture their shock...picture their tears...and I could only hope that they would hug each other a little extra for me.

I barely noticed Erik's return through the curtain of my tears, and his arms were around me almost instantly. "Oh, my dear...I wish there were words I could say or a song I could sing to truly take your pain away...But it's the proof of your love...and there is no substitute..."

"Just holding me like this suffices..." I sniffled.

"I'm glad...Although we should move on before the workers arrive..." He soothingly ran his hand up and down my spine.

"True..." I wiped at my tears, pulling back just enough so that he could take the reins.

"I have a thought....How far from here will the resort be?"

"Not far...a few miles..." Decision made, Erik coaxed the horses forward. I braved one last look at the unfinished house before letting the role of navigator distract me from my inner turmoil. We made a couple of stops downtown to get fixings for a picnic lunch when my appetite should ever return, and then we crossed the river, driving past the little boarding school I'd always admired the historical character of before turning down the road on which the resort would one day stand.

The particular overlook above the adjacent future golf course on which the exact building would be was still uncleared of trees, but Erik managed to drive the carriage far enough in so as to not attract attention. Once stopped, he pulled me close so that I could let the remainder of my pent-up tears flow. When they were finally spent, I dozed off to the sound of Erik humming a soothing rendition of Masquerade, waking up over an hour later to find him busy with his artwork. This time, I was close enough to wrap one arm around him before resting my chin upon his shoulder, sneaking a peek as I struggled to wake up fully.

I recognized the picture instantly, and my emotions threatened to bubble up all over again. Right before my eyes, he was recreating the setting of the unit's living room from memory perfectly, showing us seated on the sofa just after we had viewed the movie together. My hand was on his scars, and his eyes were closed; he was now filling in the tears that had fallen from my touch. Rather than succumbing to my own tears, I gently traced his scars with my lips, rubbing his shoulder. "You remember that...?"

"I could never forget..." He turned his face so he could meet my lips with his. "It was my very first clue as to your feelings for me..."

"Back in my time, someone came up with the concept of love languages. I figured out that physical touch is mine..."

"I don't doubt that for one moment..." Erik chuckled softly, kissing me again before gently pulling me into his arms. "What would mine be?"

"Touch is definitely a factor..." I played with his collar as I thought it over. "But I would say yours is mostly acts of service and gifts..."

"Tell me more..." He pulled my fingers to his lips.

"You're very generous with your gifts and talents...Everything you have, you share..." I held up the rose trinket that I still wore fondly around my neck. "Even when we were barely friends..."

"I just wanted to give you some happiness in that darkness I'd tried to imprison you in..." He traced my scars with his knuckle. "That hope you had was stronger than my bitterness...it saved us both..."

"We both know Who gets the credit for that, my love..." I smiled against his gentle hand that was now at rest, save for his thumb lightly circling my cheek.

"Of course, but you chose to live it out, as hard as I made it, you fought to reject the chains that I thought were my only future...fought my darkness...You chose to teach me by your example..."

"Mm...I might just have to add 'words of affirmation' onto your list of love languages..." I teased, giggling around the lump in my throat.

"It's interesting, my dear...Most of the time when it comes to languages, we teach it to others. It would seem in the case of these love languages, they teach *us* how to love..."

"And how to be loved..." I murmured as our lips met again.

We spent the remainder of the daylight hours on that wooded overlook that was now a location almost sacred to our relationship...The spot where it all started, and yet its story was one only he and I, and one day my family, would ever know. Occasionally, we snacked on the picnic lunch fixings. Mostly we remained in each other's arms, listening to the birds singing music that accompanied the wordless expressions of our love or floated through the background of our dreams as we dozed.

When the setting sun finally beckoned us from behind the trees, we made our way back into town, still snuggled up on the carriage seat as if we were newlyweds. Although we had decided to take supper in our room and turn in early, music from the newly constructed bandstand in the center of main street prompted us to delay those plans; neither of us felt the need to suggest it as Erik simply pulled the carriage up to the railing surrounding the tiny park.

As I experienced the historical moment, my mind drifted ahead to my time when summer concerts would be performed weekly as inspired by this brass band and its conductor. Mercifully, my mind did not linger on the future as my eyes fell upon the various other couples in the audience; feeling my husband's arm around me only deepened the romantic mood we were already in before the music added to it. Now, I closed my eyes with a smile, feeling my heart beat right along to the tapping of his fingers on my shoulder as he kept in time to each number. I wondered silently if he'd want to stay and chat with the conductor afterwards, but as the air chilled slightly, he wrapped his jacket tighter around me before kissing my forehead. "Let's get you to bed...you've had quite a day..."

"Are you sure? I don't mind staying..."

"We can hear them from the comfort of our room, my dear...I insist..." Knowing I wouldn't be able to argue with him this time, I simply nodded, allowing him to guide the carriage the rest of the way down main street. The next day we would be on the train again, traveling north to the mountains, and so there was indeed good reason behind his insistence. As I felt Erik's arms securely around me before drifting off to sleep an hour later, I was truly grateful; were I alone, surely my mind would once again wander and stir up the morning's anguish. Instead, I snuggled closer into him, sending up a silent but heartfelt prayer of thankfulness as the distant band's final numbers faded into the background.

****

I was awakened mid-morning two days later by a loud clap of thunder overhead. Startled rudely out of my dreams, I sat straight up in bed. "Erik...?" My eyes darted around the dimly-lit room, but the only reply I got was the sound of heavy rain splattering against the windows. I shook off the lingering sleepiness, but remained lightheaded from the shock of waking up so suddenly. I was never one to fear thunderstorms very much, but my husband's absence heightened the room's darkness and my every emotion. Lightning flashed then, and I closed my tear-filling eyes against it. "Oh, Lord, I know I'm not alone, but...where could he be..?" My imagination threatened to drift to every worst possibility, and I sniffled, hugging Erik's pillow to my chest. "Oh, I'm being silly...he's not alone either...wherever he is, he's under

Your watchful care...He had his reasoning, and the last thing he needs is for me to make him feel guilty..." Filled with a fresh wave of peace, I dried my tears, looking around the room again until my gaze fell on a tea cart that had been brought in at some point earlier that morning. Its covered trays sent a signal to my appetite; this time, Erik had mercifully left my wheelchair right beside the bed. *He's learning*... I managed a giggle before easing myself into it. Fittingly, the storm seemed to move off slightly as my confidence grew. "Thank You, Father..." I let out a relieved sigh, lifting the cover off of one of the trays.

I had barely gotten two bites in when the door flung open, revealing a very drenched, but smirking, husband of mine. "I knew you'd start without me...!" Before I could decide on which tone to counter him with, he placed a large wrapped box on the armchair next to mine.

"Goodness, Erik! Whatever this is surely could have waited til after the storm..."

"The clouds didn't open up until after I was already out getting it..." Erik shrugged, peeling off his jacket before going to fetch a towel. "And it was far too wonderful a secret for me to come up with an excuse to fetch it while you were awake." He planted a kiss on my cheek before sitting down across from me. "Well, go ahead...it won't unwrap itself..."

"You really are something else..." I giggled at his excitement that seemed so oblivious to his soaked condition. "If only I could capture how you look right now..." I shook my head, undoing the paper and strings. Lifting the box's lid, my hands came to a stop in disbelief.

"Funny you should say that..." Erik's smirk grew as I lifted out the new camera. "I put the order in while we were still in New York...I instructed them to deliver it here..." He helped me get it set up. "Go on...capture how I look right now..." He turned the chair, posing eagerly at the edge of the seat. I took the picture, somehow managing to do so with steady hands while giggling and weeping happily. I then fell into his arms, leaving a trail of kisses all over his face.

"You really are something else..." I echoed myself in a whisper, snuggling against him.

"I know how much you enjoy taking pictures outdoors...I couldn't allow you to miss the opportunities while we're here..." He broke a piece off of a muffin, lovingly feeding it to me. "And once this rain clears, I expect there will be plenty of them."

"Look at you, all optimistic..." I placed some of the muffin into his mouth as well. "And here I was, starting to let the storm get to me..."

"I've told you, my dear, you mustn't shame yourself for feeling a little bit of the darkness I once embraced. What matters is you're at peace now...as am I...we didn't let it win..." He brushed a lock of hair out of my face. "Feeling that darkness only reminds us we're human...and that we need His Light..." At that, I playfully wrinkled my nose at him.

"I'm pretty certain I've told you that sometime before...I just can't place an exact moment when I would have said it..."

"Am I not allowed to borrow the wise words of my own wife?" He gasped mockingly, and I jokingly tossed one end of the towel onto his head.

"You are. Putting words in my *mouth*, however..." I challenged, and in retort he gently shoved a larger portion of the pastry between my parted lips.

"And that muffin is all you may accuse me of putting in your mouth!" Laughing at his own joke, he returned me to the wheelchair before conveniently seeing the sudden urgent need to change out of his wet clothes. If the inner housekeeper of mine hadn't stopped me, I certainly would have thrown the rest of that muffin at his head. I instead opted to tuck away my turn for playful vengeance to be taken later on; given the mood Erik was in, I was sure I wouldn't have to wait too long.

As he had predicted, once the clouds cleared by mid-afternoon, we deemed the weather nice enough for us to venture out. Erik rented us a rowboat, and soon we were in the middle of Profile Lake, right below the natural stone 'face' of the Old Man of the Mountain. When discussing our excursion to my home state, Erik had asked me what else I wanted to see besides Plymouth. Although I had numerous options to choose from, I decided that after visiting a town full of memories, we would both need the wide-open clarity that Franconia Notch would have to offer. Being surrounded by the mountains, forests, and small bodies of water would do us a lot of good, both to sooth my emotions and to get our creative juices flowing.

My other reason was sheer curiosity; just as the Pemigewasset Hotel would cease to exist by the time I was born, so would the Profile House where we were staying. What I discovered was a slight yet deep sense of sadness I couldn't show to a single soul; I didn't even want to share it with Erik. I knew he would offer me comfort, but I wanted him to fully enjoy our time here without the cloud of impending doom hanging over him each time he looked at the structure or admired the exquisite details and decor. No, it was best that I keep it to myself that even though these buildings were not there in my time, now that I was here, I couldn't imagine losing such beautiful architecture and history.

"The lighting's perfect now, if you want a photo..." Erik pointed towards the stone face, shaking me from my thoughts.

"You're absolutely right!" I grinned, readying the camera.

"Best you remember that..." He teased with a wink.

"Are you implying an upcoming argument?" I raised an eyebrow as I took the picture.

"Not unless you care to invent one just so we can make peace with each other after..." Erik smirked, resting the oars so he could pull out his drawing pad.

"Clever way to drop the subject.." I pointed accusingly, but I knew that once he got started on an art piece, there was no pursuing any conversation. It was just as well; at that very moment, I caught a glimpse of an eagle just in time to see it land in a tree right on the water's edge. "Hold still, you..." I mumbled, getting my camera ready and zooming in on the subject. "Perfect..." I clicked the shutter victoriously, then settled back to enjoy the atmosphere. The warmth of the sun and the rocking motion of the boat were more than enough of a combination to lull me to sleep, but I fought against it, not wanting to miss a single moment or detail in the beauty of our surroundings. I instead turned my focus upward to watching the drifting clouds shift into various shapes, each one lingering for far too short of a time for me to bother with my camera or even point out to Erik.

When I finally did look his way again, I realized he was catching glances at me as he drew. I rolled my eyes, despite the flattered grin that now spread across my face. "Oh, Erik, honestly...of all the subjects you could choose out here...Haven't you done enough of me?"

"Not in this setting..." He responded without missing a beat or even smirking at my exasperation, as if he were waiting for me to notice so that he could pounce with his reply. I knew there was nothing I could do except hold still until he was finished, and so I returned my gaze to the clouds, resisting the urge to even stretch for one moment.

Finally, he slid the drawing pad onto my lap just as I was once again tempted to doze off. Looking down at the finished work, tears replaced sleep as the biggest threat. Erik had captured me in my reclined position, looking up at the clouds. What shocked me, however, was the fact that he'd drawn a childhood version of myself beside me, following my upward gaze and pointing finger. "E–Erik...h–how did...where did you get the idea to...a–and you captured my younger self so perfectly, but–"

"I partially guessed. Mostly, though, I took from how Claire looked at that age and how you looked when we first met..." Erik carefully moved so he could sit beside me. "As for the idea, all I had to see was the wonder on your face to get the inspiration. That expression of awe is simply ageless..."

"Just when I think I've seen the extent of your artistry..." I sniffled, biting my lip before kissing him tenderly. Several moments passed before he slowly pulled back, but he remained next to me as he flipped the drawing pad to the next blank page.

"I shall *now* capture the scenery..." He picked up the charcoal.

"Could...you teach me...?" The thought had danced around in my head countless times prior, but I surprised even myself with voicing the suggestion. I could feel him studying my face for a few moments before slipping the charcoal into my hand. Positioning us so that he was diagonally behind me, he took hold of the charcoal with me.

"Tell me what you see...describe every detail...shading, texture...we'll capture it together..."

Our hands moving as one across the paper was a level of intimacy I never knew could exist. My eyes and my words, and his practiced, capable hand were now totally dependent on each other in a synchronized dance upon the page, like partners first meeting and yet needing no rehearsal. After the first few glances down, I realized I could keep my eyes on the surroundings, releasing control of the charcoal into his hand's guidance. Only the sensation of his fingers wrapped around my own reminded me that I was still holding on. In turn, his chin resting on my shoulder told me that he never once looked up to verify my observations.

A soft kiss to my neck and a caress to my hand signaled the completion of our artistic experiment. "We're quite the duo, my dear..." he whispered against my ear.

"It appears so..." I giggled a bit, unable to take my eyes away from the lines and smudges that represented my descriptions. Even where I had failed to come up with the right words, he seemed to know exactly what I was trying to say and incorporated it seamlessly.

"I'll give you more formal lessons when we return home, if you'd like." He set the pad and charcoal aside, wrapping his arms around me fully.

"I'd like that..." I nodded, leaning back against him. "And more of this..." I motioned to the finished product. "And this..." I turned my head so I could let my lips show him exactly what I was talking about.

****

The photograph of the eagle supposedly captured by me in this chapter. In actuality, this was indeed captured by me at a different lake after completing this story.

****SEVEN****

The next couple of days were spent with roughly the same blend of activities; boating, writing, photography, and drawing. Several times, I caught Erik eying the mountain tops almost longingly. He always shook it off as soon as I thought to say anything, but those moments always reminded me that he had never experienced a mountain-top view. It had been my third, silent reason for suggesting this trip, but of course our plans were made before the shipwreck. To hold him back just because I was unable to join him, however, would be selfish.

Late one afternoon, I decided not to wait to catch him looking at the surrounding summits. "Erik, my love?" I made certain to keep my tone casual. "You know what picture I'd love to get?"

"Tell me..." He gave the oars one more push before letting the boat glide towards shore.

"The view from the top of that mountain..." I pointed to the ridge above us. "I'd love for you to take the picture for me..." At that, he slowed the boat and leaned forward.

"What are you suggesting, precisely...?" He raised an eyebrow. "If the picture is so important to you, I can carry you..."

"All that way? In addition to the camera and your own supplies? Absolutely not!" I scoffed, reaching forward to take his hands. "The truth is, I've been to the tops of mountains many times...I want you to experience it...the sheer exhilaration and bliss as the view takes your breath away...It's a feeling I don't want you to miss this opportunity to have..." He studied me for a bit, then smiled knowingly.

"Here I thought I was being subtle with my curiosity..."

"I'm afraid you've gone without a mask for so long, you've just lost that touch..." I shrugged teasingly.

"Oh, have I now?" He growled, pulling me over into his lap. "You should be careful about voicing such observances, my dear...Pandora's Box can always be opened..."

"Well perhaps that's exactly what I wanted..." I smirked against his lips.

"Oh, well then, forbid me to ever disappoint you..." His eyes flashed and danced as his face took on the very same expression of madness as towards the end of the movie, except this time it was entirely playful.

"Well you *are* forbidden..." I giggled around another kiss. "I've missed this side of you..."

"You needed only to say as much before...Now you must wait until we return to our room..."

"Oh? You mean there's even more to this side of you?" I teased him again, playing with his collar.

"Much more..." He growled again, nibbling gently on my ear. "Be only too glad you're still injured...I'll be forced to restrain myself..."

"Well then, I can't wait until I'm fully healed..." I pecked his lips before handing him the oars.

****

Early the next morning, Erik set out on his trek, but not before we shared breakfast and he made sure I was all set up for a day of reading and writing in the drawing room. I distracted myself from his absence by writing letters to each of the children, as well as postcards to the Girys and DeChagneys. Once the last was written, I tucked them away unsealed in case Erik wished to add anything, then wheeled myself over to the bookshelves. Selecting two novels, I moved to one of the sofas and settled myself into a relaxing position with every intention of reading.

    Instead, as more and more fellow guests trickled in, I found myself focusing more and more on people-watching, wondering what mark each one might make on history or at the very least what their stories were. It was a habit of mine ever since I took up writing, and so I failed to notice right away that I was being wondered about as well, so lost in my imaginings that I'd become. But as the whispers became clearer, I realized for the first time exactly what Erik had been subjected to...the ridicule and shame...the feeling of not belonging...

    My hand immediately went up to my scars then as burning tears rolled down my face. *It's different when it happens to you...* His words now echoed through my mind; in my stubbornness and desire to prove him wrong, I'd refused to accept any negative train of thought in regards to my new appearance. I'd been in such denial that I hadn't allowed myself time to really think it over or prepare for the shunning I was now receiving.

    Suddenly, I couldn't breathe. Somehow I managed to transfer myself back into my chair and wheel myself out to the garden. It was chilly and the wind was blowing steadily, but I didn't care; it felt wonderful and it was keeping everyone else inside. As an added bonus, the wind also drowned out my sobs as I prayed out all my frustration at myself for caring what the other guests were saying about me. There were only two other opinions that should ever matter to me besides my own. That's how it had always been. But perhaps always having Erik near to me had served as a buffer. Perhaps there had been whispers and stares the whole time we'd been in New York, and I had simply been lost in his presence that I just didn't notice.

I was certainly missing his presence now, I sniffled as the bitter thought threatened to take root. I had no cause to feel such resentment towards him, however. It had been my own idea...my own insistence that had pushed him up that mountain. No, today's temporary separation was to do us both some good; he would get the experience, and I would get the photograph. In the meantime, I was now determined to find my own joy despite the whispers.

As soon as my mind was set upon a new focus, the wind quieted ever so slightly, and a little hummingbird appeared at the flowering bush beside me. *Thank You, Father...* I lifted up a silent prayer, my smile warming me from the chilly air. With newfound courage and peace rising up inside me, I returned to the drawing room, only to be stopped by one of the bellhops as he handed me the books I'd selected. "The ladies in there said you forgot these, Madame Dupree...They thought you might have retired to your room..."

"Thank you. No, I just needed some air..." I smiled gratefully at him before attempting to continue through the doorway, but he stopped me again, clearing his throat.

"Perhaps you would be more comfortable in your room...I know how those ladies can be toward those like–that is, towards anyone who–"

"Doesn't measure up to their standards of perfection?" I broke in, watching the relief sweep over his face. "And who is to say *their* standard is perfect? No, to hide myself away would be to feed the lie they tell themselves and each other that they are allowed to exclude anyone, albeit passively. I was foolish for surrendering to them just now...I'd much rather return to that sofa."

"Of course, Madame..." He smiled kindly, his eyes dancing with amusement at this rebellious act against society's petty vanity. Practically marching as he pushed my chair to the sofa, he collected a few more throw pillows to prop me up even more comfortably than before. "Shall I bring you some tea?"

"That would be lovely, thank you..." I nodded, resisting the urge to watch the reactions of the others. "Instead, I opened the first novel, listening as the gasps and whispers faded and turned to other topics of discussion when they finally realized I'd not been defeated. *Lord I pray they never have to experience such scars firsthand, but grant them compassion and softened hearts. Help them to see through Your eyes...*

"Madame Dupree?" The voice was gentle, but urgent enough for me to glance up from my book. The room had dimmed and was empty now, aside from myself and the kind bellhop from before.

"What time is it?" I set the book down with a stretch, only now realizing how stiff my joints had become.

"Nearing half past six...You looked so involved in your book I didn't want to disturb you, but I don't want you to miss supper."

"Oh..." I straightened up, taking a peek out the window at the darkening sky. "I thought my husband would be back down the mountain by now..."

"I wouldn't worry too much, Madame...It's easy for one to lose track of time or other plans. I've seen it happen quite often. It's like with your books...you find yourself immersed in a whole other world entirely..."

"I know what you mean..." I mumbled with a sigh, straightening my dress.

"It might take him longer to descend without the light of day. It's easy to lose the trail in the dark." At that, I let out a subtle laugh.

"Not *my* husband..."

"Oh..?" The younger man helped me into my chair.

"There was a time...in fact a good portion of his life...where he lived in the darkness...found it comforting...embraced it. I doubt that even after all these years, he's lost that instinct and ability entirely. No, he'll find his way sure enough..."

"Of course. Still, if it makes you feel better, we have a small crew at the ready to form a search party if it gets to be too late. They go out almost regularly to guide missing hikers back."

"Thank you..." I nodded. "In the meantime, I'd better eat something...In my room, preferably. You've looked after me more than enough today already."

"Oh, it's no trouble at all, Madame. You remind me of my mother...I haven't seen her in some time, and so it does me good to help." He tipped his hat slightly. "Even so, if you truly wish to take supper in your room, I won't stop you."

"Thank you again..." I took note of his nametag. "Charlie...more than anything, it just wouldn't feel right having supper in the dining room unaccompanied..."

"Of course...I should have thought..."

"Never you mind. You've restored my sense of belonging all the more. Thank you."

"I was only doing my duty as a fellow human being, Madame..." He smiled politely before wheeling me to my room. Once I had my supper, I slipped a few coins into his hand. After assuring me I'd be kept updated as to Erik's whereabouts, he left me to my own company. I refused to let my mind wander, however. Purposefully focusing on eating, changing, and climbing into bed, I lifted up one more prayer for Erik before willing myself to sleep restfully.

****

    I stared into the bathroom mirror, past my tears into the face of my younger self. I was back in that resort unit, the years erased as if I'd never left. The life we had built together had died with him a century ago, and yet the memories we'd shared were still crystal clear. In desperation, my fingers searched futilely for the rose trinket; even that had been taken away. My head spun with questions and confusion, and I tightened my grip on the edges of the sink to keep myself from collapsing. *It can't be. There were no trips left. Surely it wasn't a mere dream...I remember so much...* Eyes burning, I fumbled my way through the doorway and lowered myself onto the closest twin bed....the very same one he'd placed me upon on that first day. Even the pages of my writings he'd tossed about were gone, as if his very existence had been my imagination. *But no...I had loved him. I still love him. I know he was here...* My mind wandered then to what he must have gone through when he discovered my sudden absence. *Does he remember me? Or was it just a dream to him too?* I sniffled, clutching the pillow to my chest as I curled up around it. *No...we had both loved and been loved...what we had was real...he was real...* "Oh, Erik..." I whimpered. "I don't want that old photograph if that mountain's just going to rip us apart....I just want you...I just want you..."

    "I'm here, Sarah..." A gentle hand brushed against my face, wiping my tears in the process. I reached up to take hold of it as I felt his other hand on my shoulder, carefully pulling me out of my sleep and into his arms. "I'm here..."

"Oh, Erik, it was awful...my deepest fear...we were parted again, by time and space...nothing but memories left as evidence of our life together..."

"And it was but a dream, my dear..." He softly kissed my forehead, then my temple, then my lips. "This is real...my arms around you...my fingers in your hair...the love we share...Time and space could do nothing to stop this love, remember?"

"Y–yes...I remember..." I sniffled again, nodding against his chest. "Just...every so often, the nagging thought of 'what if' rises up in my mind...and last night..."

"I should have been here..." He sighed, laying down on his back but still holding me close on top of him. As his hand moved soothingly up and down my spine, he rested his lips against the top of my head. "You were right, though. That view was an experience I needed to have...The hours passed like mere seconds as I was up there, capturing it on paper and with the camera... Every way I possibly could...I still don't think I did it justice..."

"I know what you mean..." I smiled up at him. "Many times, back in my time, I would look at the pictures I took afterwards and they just didn't strike me the same way..." I shifted slightly so I could reach up and caress his face comfortingly. "Still, I'm glad you got to see and feel what it's like up there...Anything you produce from it will be worth it knowing you got that chance. Don't let my nightmare prompt even a drop of regret on your memory of it." We both fell silent then, letting our fingers and lips converse for the moment. "What time is it, anyway?" I glanced at the window, but the closed curtains told me nothing.

"Early enough that we can still get a decent amount of sleep..." He brushed my hair out of my face. "Unless you're too awake now..."

"I am, but I can easily return to sleep in your arms. You need it..."

"I won't argue with that..." He chuckled softly, carefully maneuvering the blankets out from underneath himself so he could tuck us both in. "I meant to tell you, my dear...one of the bellhops, Charlie, led the search party that met me a little ways up the trail. He mentioned your unspoken concern, despite your brave front, and how you handled the gossip in the drawing room. I'm proud of you..."

"I almost let it win..." I sighed.

"But you came out the winner. 'Almost' is a powerful barrier of a word...Don't sell yourself short..."

"Mm...but I *am* short, though..." I teased, poking fun at my own lack of height. My joke prompted him to tickle me in response.

"Congratulations, my dear...I've just caught my second wind..." He growled, kissing me with a fresh wave of energy.

The early morning fog enveloped me
As I climbed from rock bottom—
A valley of sorrow
Clouds and misty tears
Stole my sight

Still, I climbed
Ever moving forward

Fingers clutching at rocks and branches
Clawing their way over gravel
At each rest stop more tempted
To stay
To return

Still, I climbed
Ever moving forward
My goal in mind

Finally, the ground levels
As I reach the summit
The fog thins, and I find myself
In a world of evergreen trees
And thick moss
Soft under my weary body

Here, I rest
Catching my breath

Only to lose it again
As the wind chases off the remaining clouds
Like a curtain rising
Revealing the view

I look back down
Upon how far I've come
The trials and the trails
Seem so small and meaningless

Here I rest
Here I reflect

No...
The journey had meaning after all...
The climb out of the valley of sorrows
There was purpose in all the pain and struggle
That made me human
Not a monster
Not a phantom
A man.
~Erik J. Dupree 1905
A Poem from the Summit of Cannon Mountain

####*EIGHT*####

    We remained at the Profile House another week, taking one day to travel by stagecoach to a town further northeast that was popular with tourists, even still in my time. There, we visited various shops, picking up souvenirs and trinkets for ourselves and for our family and close friends. As much as we enjoyed the long-overdue 'alone time' portion of our honeymoon, it was good to get back on the train bound for New York, knowing the familiar faces that would be waiting. This time, we bypassed Plymouth and any other stopovers; I was more than satisfied with the explorations we had already embarked on. No, we would be returning to France soon enough, and we both were eager to spend as much time with Janelle's family before then as possible.

    Over a late celebratory dinner with them upon our arrival, we were informed that Ethan's adoption had become official, but Helaine had not been able to secure employment. We then told her of our idea, which she was more than happy to agree to. Erik and I exchanged a secret look of relief and strengthened hope for our son's happiness then.

    The remaining weeks of our time in America were spent much like before. However, we did less sightseeing, choosing instead to accompany Janelle to the opera house for rehearsals or on shopping excursions, or Samuel to the harbor for the occasional ferry ride. The most noteworthy outing was opening night of Janelle's newest performance. As we were heading toward our private box, who should be wheeled through the doors of the opera house but Carlotta herself! Watching Erik's face, I saw shock turn to borderline protest. It soon softened with compassion, however, as he saw Carlotta's tearful hesitation, taking in all the surroundings and memories that surely came with them. He shocked us all, perhaps even himself, by being the first to approach her. "Carlotta...welcome...did Janelle know you were coming?"

"*Bonta*, no! I was not even certain myself up until I arrived! I did not wish to get her hopes up..."

"She'll be thrilled..." He gave her an assuring smile. "You must join us..."

"You do not want that..." She scoffed dismissively.

"I insist..." As an added measure to convince the both of them, he took it upon himself to wheel her forward. Lydia broke from Samuel's side, gripping her grandmother's hand with unrestrained enthusiasm. With Joseph taking her other hand, Erik almost didn't need to push her chair along the corridor to the lift, but he did anyway; perhaps he needed to be holding on to either steady himself or to remind himself that this was indeed actually happening. Samuel took up the task of pushing mine, and Ethan hobbled beside us, fully capable of keeping up the pace with little help from Helaine.

Once in our box, there was almost no discussion of seating arrangements. Ethan chose to sit between Helaine and Erik, who placed Carlotta on the other side of me from him. Lydia planted herself on the former diva's lap, leaving the remaining two seats next to her for Samuel and Joseph. As we waited for the show to begin, we filled Carlotta in on our travels up north. She seemed persuaded that the fresh mountain air would do her health and spirits some good, and Samuel agreed to plan a trip the following year for them all.

With that, we settled back as the theater darkened, our focus turning to the opening curtain below. As usual, Janelle lit up the stage with both her talent and her genuine warmth toward all who shared it with her. Although the entire audience was captured by her presence, when it came time for the curtain call, the loudest applause came from our box; even Carlotta was able to muster enough strength to match our volume and enthusiasm. It was enough for Janelle to look our way, clearly shocked and touched to see her mother watching. Erik readied to toss the bouquet of roses we'd brought, but at the last moment he handed it to Carlotta to throw to the stage. The former diva smiled graciously at his gesture, taking only half before handing the rest back. The flowers landed with expert precision at Janelle's feet, next to the ones Samuel had already thrown.

As the others prepared to go backstage, I took hold of Erik's arm. "You all go ahead...We'll join you momentarily..." Knowing we would follow through, they nodded and exited the box, Samuel taking the position behind his mother-in-law's wheelchair. Before Erik could question me, I carefully stood, keeping all my weight on my good leg as I wrapped my arms around him, kissing him deeply. He matched the kiss with no hesitation, not seeming to care I had yet to give a reason. "You were so wonderful...I'm proud of you..."

"I wish I could take credit, to be deserving of such an embrace..." He chuckled, taking a seat but holding me sideways on his lap. "The truth is, I didn't have a chance to act as I normally would...It was as instinctual as breathing, what actually occurred...I could not have stopped myself if I'd tried..."

"But you don't regret it..." I smoothed his tie and collar. "I can see it in your eyes..."

"I do feel quite good about it..." He nodded, planting a soft kiss on my temple. "My old self would have been disgusted with my actions..."

"Your old self is gone, though I loved him just the same..." I rested my head on his shoulder. "You've come a long way since then, though, and I wouldn't change a single thing..."

"Mm...there is *one* part of my old self that still exists, that you would hate to see die off completely..." He smirked, his eyes dancing mischievously.

"How dare you even make me think of such a notion!" I gasped playfully.

"Just to show you that it's still very much alive..." He chuckled, pressing his lips against mine. "Now, shall we join the others before they come looking?"

"You tease!" I lightly smacked his shoulder, feeling red heat rise to my cheeks. "You are right though....but the night is still young..." I straightened myself, allowing him to return me to my chair.

"That it is, my dear..." He kissed me once more before wheeling me toward the lift. "That it is..."

****

For our final full day in New York, we decided to visit Coney Island. Erik was hesitant when it was described as a giant fair, but when he saw the excitement of the younger ones, he gave in. Of the three adjacent but separate parks, we chose to spend our time in Dreamland; it seemed to offer the most family-friendly variety so that we'd all be sure to have a fun time.

Once Erik saw all the rides and amusements, and the fact that he could absolutely participate finally sank in, he completely released his inner child, the one that could never truly experience the simple joys and innocent playtime that every childhood needs to have. Although I was unable to join him on the faster rides, I was content just to watch his face; I couldn't capture it with my camera, but I knew the image would be engraved in my memory. The carefree laughter and shrieks brought me back to our days as young parents, watching him run around with and entertain our children. I recalled with such fondness how they would play a sort of hide-and-seek, and how he would have to tone down his old Opera Ghost self so as to not frighten or frustrate them. And then there were the times when he himself was the thrill ride; when Antoin or Claire would beg him to carry them on his back and trot around like a horse or fly them through the air so they could feel like birds. Surely they exhausted him with their endless requests, but he never once let them know it.

Now, there was no weariness in his face. Even as the three youngest scrambled to cling tightly to him as the roller coaster flew downward, hindering his view by covering his eyes instead of theirs in their franticness, his smile only grew wider. His laughter was contagious; soon Helaine was also giggling beside me at the sight. When the coaster carried them out of view, I glanced over at her. "You know, you really don't have to sit out every ride just because I am, Helaine..."

"Oh, I don't mind. My stomach can't take much excitement." There was something deeper going on behind the smile she threw at me, but I decided to not pursue it just then.

"Just so long as you're enjoying yourself..."

"Oh, I am...thank you, Madame Dupree.." The shadow retreated deeper inside her, hidden by her candidness. "I never really had much chance to go to a fair growing up. Just being here, seeing everything...it's more than enough..."

"I'm glad..." I hesitated a moment, gathering my thoughts. "In a way, this is my husband's first experience as well..."

"I thought he said he grew up in a fair..."

"He did…but he never got to enjoy it like he is now…not even close…"

"Oh, that's true…" she bit her lower lip, "I suppose, while the grass may seem greener on the other side of the fence, in reality the green is just along the fence itself. Beyond it lies a desert…"

"But when we let love in, it breaks down the fence, nourishing the land with healing tears and the light of hope…"

"I can see that in the both of you…" she smiled sweetly.

"You, too, have that healing love inside of you, Helaine…Sooner or later, God will show you the barren land that needs what you offer."

"Perhaps…" her cheeks reddened at the mention of that dream possibly coming true for her. "Until then, I'm so grateful I'll be living under the example of your relationship."

"And I'm grateful for your company and assistance." I gave her arm a gentle squeeze as the rest of our party joined us. Erik's eyes were still wide with amusement as he kissed me in greeting.

"I noticed a house of mirrors from the ride…shall we go there next?"

"Of *course* you'd suggest such a thing…" I giggled, my comment met with a flash of his old self forbidding me to say anything further that would spoil his fun. "To the house of mirrors then!" I failed to suppress a knowing smirk as I motioned us forward. Once again, I was unable to go in with my wheelchair, but I did convince Helaine to go along with the others. Erik made sure he was the last to enter, winking at me confidently before disappearing.

Sure enough, he was the first one out, darting back to the entrance. Three times, he circled back, each time guiding first Lydia and Joseph, then Ethan and Helaine, and finally Janelle and Samuel. Each rescue seemed to increase his playfulness and energy; never before had I seen him so at ease and thoroughly happy.

Little did any of us know how short-lived his happiness would be that day. If we had, we would have left shortly after. Instead, we followed the sound of a sudden commotion a few yards away. Ethan spoke up first, his streetwise trained ear immediately picking up what was going on. "Sounds like a fight!" he announced, instinctive curiosity carrying him towards it before we could stop him; how fast he'd become with those crutches of his!

"Ethan, no!" Samuel darted after him.

"You ladies stay with the children..." Erik growled, seeming to know something more about the fight than the rest of us could. As the men divided the crowd in front of us, I caught a glimpse of a fist fight between two dwarves right in the middle of the street. It didn't seem like it was for show; surely there would have at least been a ring roped off around them. Just as Samuel finally caught up to Ethan and gently pulled him back, the stronger fighter's fist made contact with the other's jaw with such force that they were both knocked off balance. The fall did nothing to distract him, however, as fists continued to fly with the crowd laughing and cheering them on.

In one swift blurry move, Erik pulled the stronger one off of the other, causing the cheers to turn to boos. Seemingly oblivious to the disapproval, he took hold of the dwarf's shoulders. "What's all this about that it can't be settled without throwing punches? Don't you know there are children around?"

"You fool! You're spoiling everything!" Meeting his glare evenly, the smaller man wiped his forearm across his bloodied lip.

"Oh am I?" Erik raised an eyebrow. "What did this man do that would require you to dole out justice yourself?" He motioned to the older one still on the ground. Not waiting for a reply, he turned toward him, kneeling to help him to his feet. Instead, his eyes widened in recognition. "Betzazel...?" Concern flooded his face, stirring his anger all the more as he turned back to the other man. "Answer me! What could he have possibly done to deserve such abuse?" He was met with a roll of the eyes as the fighter leaned closer, his voice a whispered hiss I could barely make out.

"Look. It's not real...it's just an act. He did nothing but his job, as did I!"

"The blood's real enough..." Erik growled, turning his attention to helping Betzazel up.

"It's just a few scrapes and bruises. We'll heal in time for the next one..." The other man scoffed, approaching Betzazel. "You know this man, Zazzie?" He jerked a thumb at Erik, at which the old performer shook his head in bewilderment.

"No...you wouldn't know me..." Erik sighed. "Not by sight...only by what I used to call myself...O.G." As he voiced his old alias, Betzazel stumbled back, almost losing his balance all over again.

"Look, you're clearly upsetting him, and you're costing us our jobs!" The younger dwarf gently took hold of Betzazel's arm. "Why don't you leave him alone?"

"You call this a job?" Erik's voice shook with emotion, showing no sign of backing down. "One or both of you could get seriously hurt, or worse! All for what? These crowds don't care if you live or die. They'll just find someone else to laugh at and mock...someone like me...They don't care that Betzazel once graced the stage at the Opera Populaire...nor that he's a gifted toymaker...a comedian who put genuine smiles on children's faces...They don't care about unique potential or hidden talents...They only care about the difference they see...Treating you and I as nothing more than a painting on a wall...A conversation piece...Not a human being!" Tears and shock flooded Betzazel's face as Erik spoke, and he tugged on my husband's sleeve to get his attention before shakily mouthing,

"You were watching?"

"Of course..." Erik offered a small smile through his own tears. "I was the Opera Ghost, after all...I saw the way you were treated...and I took it upon myself to punish Piangi for it..." At his confession, Betzazel hung his head, remembering his old friend. By now, the disgruntled crowd had dispersed to find something else to amuse them, allowing the rest of us to move a little bit closer. "I was wrong, Betzazel. You clearly loved him like a brother, willing to look past his faults...The world should only learn from your example..." Erik placed a comforting hand on the dwarf's shoulder. "If I had known what my actions would do to you...your future..." He shook his head, sighing. "That I was pushing you towards a life I myself fled from..."

"It's not all that bad..." The other dwarf spoke up dismissively. "We've got our own city of sorts...everything built to fit our size...Houses, stores, even our own fire department..." He motioned to a nearby sign for the 'Midget City'. "Most of the time, we're so caught up in our every day lives, we don't even notice the crowd..."

"And yet they are there, aren't they?" Erik's eyes flashed with old anger once again. "Watching your every move as if your lives were a mere puppet show...it only confirms to them the ridiculous notion that anyone who looks different has no place in society except to amuse them! Staged fires...fistfights in the streets...They won't be laughing and cheering when someone really does get hurt in a situation *they* demanded to see in the first place! You're settling for less than you deserve...far less. I just hope someday you realize that...before it's too late..."

"Look, it's not like we're locked up like prisoners! We signed up for it and we can leave whenever we want. The fact is, they're gonna laugh and stare no matter where we go. We might as well get paid for it, right, Zazzie?" He lightly elbowed his friend's ribs, resulting in Betzazel's face twisting in pain.

"You really are hurt..." Erik mumbled, not an ounce of accusation toward the other dwarf in his voice. Hearing the genuine compassion, Betzazel looked up at Erik and nodded, almost pouting.

"Let's get you to the doctor..." The other fighter started toward Midget City, but Betzazel stopped him with a firm tug of the arm. Shaking his head with fresh determination, he mouthed, "No more..."

"What do you mean, Zazzie? You heard him, you're hurt!"

"Not that one..." Betzazel mouthed, motioning to the park exit. "Real..."

"What, you're just gonna quit? Your life is here! I mean, this is *me* you're dealing with...Your buddy Ralphie...You're just gonna listen to this...old acquaintance who only now decided to act like he cares about you?"

"I want to make toys again..." Betzazel silently explained. "He reminded me. No more fights."

"So you can make toys here! I'm sure the bosses can get you a shop..." Again, Ralphie was met with furious head-shaking in response, and Erik decided to give voice to his observation.

"You don't understand. In here, all they'll see is yet another novelty to amuse them...They won't take his work seriously. Out there, shoppers expect their purchases to have the quality he can deliver. Here, they'll line up demanding something on-the-spot...His toys would lose that extra, personal element he usually puts in. You just can't put that level of dedication and care on display or at factory speed." Betzazel's eyes watered all over again at Erik's vote of confidence.

"They'll still stare..." Ralphie scoffed stubbornly.

"I expect they will at first..." Erik relented slightly. "But his talent will change their focus. That's one thing my wife has helped me to see...We're much more than our differences...but if all we focus on are those things that set us apart, they will imprison us. When we instead decide to discover what we can truly offer, and realize that we're all equally human, we find freedom and the confidence to explore all sorts of possibilities until we find our rightful place in this world."

"Go on then! *My* place is here!" Ralphie waved them both off, not even bidding farewell before marching off toward the Midget City gates. Samuel and Erik then helped Betzazel get a carriage to the hospital and left a note with him to give to his next driver that would bring him to Janelle's home afterward. Upon their return, we all silently agreed to somehow regain the sense of fun we'd been having up til that encounter.

The three youngest seemed to recover faster, spotting a booth selling ice cream. We all got in line, and then Erik and I brought our cones to a bench overlooking the water. He seemed to forget his surroundings almost immediately, melting ice cream dripping down onto his still-trembling hand. Frowning, I placed my handkerchief over the vanilla streaks, giving his hand a gentle squeeze in the process. "Have I lost you to the past again, my love?" At the sound of my voice, the dam holding back his emotions burst. Grabbing both cones, I wrapped my free arm around him, pulling his head to my shoulder.

"I should have done more...I couldn't make him see th–the danger...the wicked greed of such displays...they're being used...enslaved...and he just didn't care!"

"You saved Betzazel, though..." I soothingly rubbed his back. "I'm so proud of you for controlling yourself...I know you were holding back..."

"And what good did it do? They'll just find more...The crowds will demand it..." His voice was weak with pain...pain that he was undoubtedly feeling to his very core. "I wanted to do more, Sarah! They deserve to see the truth! But...I just...I couldn't bring myself to do it...as much as I tried, I just couldn't!"

"It's because you've come so far away from your old self...The new has pushed those old violent outbursts into complete banishment. You're much more mature and at peace. Don't you see? You didn't fail to shine the light of truth, my love. They just weren't ready to let go..."

"Do you think they'll ever be?" He sniffled, his eyes meeting mine, tearfully searching for hope.

"Perhaps..." I smiled gently. "Maybe Betzazel's continued absence will cause Ralphie to take your words to heart."

"I hope so, Sarah....I really do..." A fresh wave of tears spilled out as he sighed, completely drained. I kissed away the drops, holding him a little tighter.

"All we can do is focus on what we can control, my love, and then give the rest over to God. He knows their need far greater than we do."

"Ever the voice of reason...." He finally smiled albeit sleepily.

"For one thing, we can control this ice cream from melting any further..." I gently teased, handing him back his dessert. It was not in the least meant to make light of his emotions; although it wasn't a brownie, I knew he'd take comfort in the sugary cold treat, which he did between a few final sniffles. Once our cones had been eaten, we just sat there, holding each other. There was no sense of urgency to rush to the next ride or amusement, and so we persuaded Helaine to go with the children and their parents to get their minds totally off of the incident. We would rejoin them at the gates in time for supper.

When we both felt ready, we went over to the replica of the Canals of Venice, where Erik paid a little extra to maneuver our gondola himself. Almost immediately, it seemed as though we had been transported to his opera house caverns from all those years ago. I was so tempted to start singing that particular song, but I wasn't sure just how he would take it. I certainly didn't want to send him reeling back emotionally all over again. He appeared to be favoring the silence for the moment anyway, and I was more than content to sit back and enjoy the experience.

Then, as if reading my mind, he quietly began singing 'No One Would Listen', changing a few words so that he was singing it to me rather than about me. I smiled and carefully leaned back against him, making sure I didn't knock him off-balance. In turn, he gave the boat one large boost before kneeling down behind me, caressing the scars on my face. "I love you, Erik...so much..." I nuzzled his hand.

"And I you..." He bent over, softly kissing me albeit upside-down. We would have sat there adrift for much longer, but another boat soon came up behind us, urging us to reluctantly continue through the canal.

When we finally met up with the others, it was decided that Samuel and Janelle would go to fetch Carlotta to join us for a final supper together, and Erik, Helaine, and I would go to the hospital to check on Betzazel. It was not our intent to make this occasion into a reunion between the two; our initial thought was to prevent Betzazel from being driven to an empty house. Thankfully, his injuries were no worse than a few bumps and bruises which would heal on their own in a matter of days, and so he was being released by the time we arrived. He seemed to be in much better spirits, having made up his mind about getting back into toy-making. We kept silent about Carlotta, and the look on both their faces once we arrived at the restaurant told us we'd made the right choice.

    I couldn't help but smile to myself as I watched them greet each other with mixed emotions and silent tears; perhaps it was mere wishful thinking on the part of Erik's romantic writer of a wife, as he so often referred to me as out of fondness, but there was something about the way they prolonged their embrace that seemed to speak of a deeper connection...Something more than their mutual love for Piangi. Even if it was just that, then perhaps in time it would grow into a love for each other. Surely in the sincerity on Carlotta's face, she would not be so quick to dismiss the dwarf from her life, and as Erik squeezed my hand under the table, I knew that he could see her tears were not from mere pity...that she truly wanted to make things right, even if it took the rest of their remaining years to do so.

****

*****NINE*****

"You will come see us in France again soon?" I clung to Janelle's hands the next morning. The air was cold and rainy as we were saying our goodbyes, doing all it could to further dampen our spirits and destroy the hope in my voice.

"Of course, Mama..." Her reassuring smile cleared the lingering cloud of doubt from my mind. "Ethan would love the adventure, and Joseph and Lydia need to have their memories refreshed of where you raised me. Perhaps I can even convince Mother and Betzazel to accompany us..."

"That would be wonderful. Try to be understanding, though, if they don't wish to confront their sad memories. Piangi meant a great deal to the both of them."

"I know..." She squeezed my hands. "And perhaps they, too, wish to have their memories refreshed, just as their friendship has been..."

"That's your Papa's wisdom rubbing off on you..." I grinned proudly, and she giggled.

"Yours, too, Mama. I thank God every day that I had you both to pour into me."

"I thank Him too, for you bringing us together..."

"Are you ready, my dear...?" Erik placed a hand on my shoulder, his voice filled with reluctance about reminding us of the time.

"I suppose I am..." I sighed, pulling Janelle into one more tight hug.

"Soon, Mama...I promise..." she whispered before pulling away. After giving hugs to the grandchildren with gentle reminders to be good for their parents, we made our way onto the ship.

    This time, Samuel and Janelle had helped us acquire a first-class suite, with an actual bed so that Erik didn't have to move mattresses and furniture. There was also a separate bedchamber for Helaine, and a fairly spacious sitting room. As we were settling in, I noticed Helaine seemed quiet but restless. "What's wrong?" I wheeled myself over to the sofa where she was sitting.

    "Oh, nothing really...I'm being silly..." She threw on a brave smile.

    "Don't dismiss your feelings if they're true, Helaine. If it matters to you, it matters to me..."

    "It's just the thought of making this entire voyage again...I know we survived the trip here from the island, but..."

    "It's completely normal to have such trepidations, dear, after what we've been through..." I cut her off with a shake of the head.

    "I promise you both, this time we'll all stick together." Erik spoke up.

    Stick together we did, through the entire voyage. Since Erik was not employed as a musician this trip, he made sure none of us went anywhere or were left behind alone. Our journey was quite uneventful; the most notable occurrence being a check-up with the ship's doctor, who cleared me to practice walking with two canes, then one. I would have to go back to two canes once we were on land, of course, until I regained my balance completely. I was so grateful to have Erik and Helaine literally beside me every step after shaky step, and gradually my legs got enough strength back so that I was able to leave my wheelchair with the ship's doctor and walk down the gangplank once we reached France.

As the hired carriage approached our house, I spotted Antoin seated on the bench out front, huddled over his sketchbook. Just as I started to smile at the picture of an artist at work, however, he angrily made a scribbling motion before tossing the book to the side. Only then did he look up and notice our arrival. Rubbing his face to seemingly push aside his turmoil just long enough to greet whoever was paying a visit, he stood up and moved toward the gate. Erik flung the carriage door open the moment we came to a stop, and Antoin's frustration disappeared completely.

"Papa! Mama!" He grinned, barely opening the gate fully before squeezing through.

"Hello, Son..." Erik hugged him before touseling his hair. "The house is still standing, I see..."

"Barely..." Antoin chuckled, returning the joke. "I very nearly sent for Claire and Henri to come save me!"

"I'm sure they wouldn't have minded, dear..." I spoke up, recognizing the partial truth in his statement. At that, he helped me down out of the carriage while carefully hugging me at the same time.

"I received your letter...I'm glad you came out of the wreck alright. You look well, though, Mama...the trip seems to have done you some good, despite your injuries..."

"Thank you, dear, it did!" I smiled. "And how did you fare? You've been eating?" I searched his face, knowing full well that both father and son would let their appetites go if ever their art refused to cooperate.

"Enough to still be standing..." He admitted with a sigh. "Cooking is not my forte..." His eyes then looked past me and fell on Helaine for the first time. "Who's this..?"

"Antoin, this is our new companion and caregiver, Helaine. She also survived the wreck..."

"Hello..." Helaine's voice was quiet with shyness, but she managed to extend her hand in greeting; Antoin in turn took hold of it to help her down.

"That's quite the task you've chosen to undertake, keeping your eyes on these two..!" He chuckled, easing her apprehension. "I'll let you in on a secret though: they'll do anything you ask if you bribe them with sweets..."

"Oh, as if you and Claire didn't follow that example!" Erik laughed, giving our son a playful shove.

"It always worked though!" I giggled. "Now you men bring our bags in and Helaine and I will whip up some brownies..."

"Right away!" The two of them scrambled to grab the luggage all at once, and Helaine helped us make our escape before they could realize they'd just fallen victim to the exact trick we'd been discussing.

Once the dessert was in the oven, I had Antoin show Helaine to Claire's old bedroom so that she could settle in. Erik came inside then, having paid the carriage driver, and I noticed Antoin's sketchbook in his hand. After flipping through a few pages, he set the book down on the table and let out a heavy sigh. Before I could question his change of mood, Antoin made his appearance. "The bowl ready to be licked, Mama? Or did Papa beat me to it?" His childlike grin faded, however, when he saw the book.

"We need to talk, Son..." Erik's eyes were already welling up with the weight of whatever was on his mind. Placing a hand on Antoin's shoulder, he pulled some chairs out for them both at the table.

"I've just lost my inspiration, Papa..." Antoin sat down, sighing.

"No...you've let Camille steal it from you. All these pieces...some I recognize from before you even met her...they're all scratched out..." Erik flipped through the pages toward the beginning of the book. "You're letting her rejection silence the part of you that created this art and found it beautiful...complete..."

"Perhaps that part of me was a fool..." Antoin muttered, slamming the book shut. "Maybe Camille just opened my eyes."

"Antoin, you're following my footsteps down the wrong path." Erik gave his shoulder a squeeze, forcing him to look up. "I held that belief myself for so long...almost preventing you and Claire from ever being born. I let my art and my music become a rope around the Vicomtesse, disguised as love. I forgot who I was before I knew her. Your art is natural...a part of you...it comes from within just as much, if not more than from what's around you. It's bigger than any box anyone might try to stow it away in. It's yours...no one else's..." He slid the book closer to Antoin, opening it to a blank page. "Camille was one part of your life...one chapter in your story. It's time to look to the next one."

"Papa, I–"

"Now, I'm not saying what you felt for her wasn't real. Same with the pain that's running deep...you're allowed to be hurt...to be angry...to grieve for your heart's loss...but, Son, true artists take those emotions and learn from them. Don't let them overtake you. Don't be so consumed by them that you miss what's right in front of you, right now. You're not alone in this. We've been there..we know. And we won't let you stay down in this pit for any longer than necessary to prepare you for that next chapter."

"Th–thank you, Papa..." Voice shaking, Antoin threw his arms around Erik, finally letting all his heartbreak out.

****

    It didn't take very long for us to settle back into being home, even with the added presence of Helaine. She seemed to fit right into the flow of things, sensing when I needed assistance before I could even ask. Antoin was in no rush to return to Paris, and we felt no urgency or desire to see him go. Now that he had allowed his emotions to escape, he in turn had more room for inspiration to enter. Almost every afternoon, he and Erik would go off on some excursion to work on their art, but I suspected that more often than not, they would take that time to chat, man-to-man as well as father-to-son. I didn't mind their absence, of course; I knew they both needed that quality time. Erik had obtained such an abundance of wisdom to pour out into his first born and his only son.

    As for my hopes for Antoin and Helaine, it was still far too early on to be encouraged or disappointed. To be sure, he treated her with polite kindness, but I knew he wasn't ready to get any closer to her. Helaine was also silent about her opinion of him, though once in a while I caught her blushing ever so slightly when he addressed her. "Patience, my little romance writer..." Erik smirked one evening when I brought up the subject.

    "I'm trying, believe me!" I giggled, fluffing up his pillow to keep my nervous hands busy while he changed for bed. "Have you...given him any hints?"

    "No, and I likely won't until he brings up the subject himself." He took the pillow from me, sitting down on the bed before wrapping his hands around mine to still them. "My dear, you yourself reminded me long ago that true love can't be forced. Theirs is not your story to write. Neither was ours, if you think of it. Had it been up to you, I would have come around a lot sooner, and had it been up to me all those years ago, I never would have met you. At the same time, had Christine held the pen, her father never would have died, nor would she have ended up at the opera house." He paused then, leaning back against the headboard before pulling me into a comforting embrace. "Don't you see? There has to be an outside writer, else our stories become a tangled mess of our own selfish desires. If they really are meant to be together, Sarah, it will happen, but only in God's perfect timing. If not, then we cannot go against His Plan. He knows best."

"I know..." I sighed, resting my head on his shoulder. "I just so much want them to be happy..."

"And they will be, when the time is right." He gently kissed my head. "But that heartbreak...that pain Antoin is feeling...it's not going to go away overnight. He needs to learn to trust again...not just Helaine, but any woman who looks his way, admires his art...He needs to find that inner peace that can only come from above. Once he does, he'll be ready for the next step."

"You really have become a wise old man, haven't you?" I teased.

"Oh, old, am I?" He raised an eyebrow, scoffing. "I'll show you just how 'old' I am!"

****

With Erik's words of wisdom in my mind, I was determined to focus on other things besides my hopes for Helaine and Antoin. Thankfully Christmastime would soon be upon us, offering plenty of distractions for me. Between decorating the house and preparing gifts for everyone, I almost completely forgot about such matters until Helaine herself raised the question of what

Antoin might like as a gift from her. It took me a few minutes to choose my words so that my reply would come across as neutral. "Well, you can never go wrong with a batch of fudge...He still thinks I don't see him sneaking extra pieces to munch on later..."

"That's very true!" She smiled somewhat distantly, her fingers fiddling with the bow she'd just added to a wreath she'd been crafting. "He certainly inherited your husband's appetite for sweets! I was thinking of something that might last a bit longer, though...Something he could use, like a scarf, but personal to him, such as a new canvas or sketchbook..."

"Those are all wonderful choices..." I let my voice fade into silence, carefully weighing the impact of what I might respond further. My answer, I finally decided, would have to depend solely on her. "Tell me, what is it you want your gift to say to him? You said you want it to last...is that from practicality or from a motive to make it memorable?"

"Both, I suppose..." She bit her lip. Several moments passed of her starting to speak but then choosing silence. I did not intend to push, and yet I could tell that whatever was burdening her would only grow heavier the longer she allowed it to fester.

"Helaine..?"

"Oh, never mind...I'll do the fudge...or I could at least wrap the box of it in a scarf..." She began to paw through the basket of yarn, looking for the right colors. I gently stopped her hand, but she didn't look up.

"That's not what you really want, is it?"

"It doesn't matter..." she sighed with a bitter, distant smile and small shake of her head. "It's not the time...perhaps it never will be...I'm just a friend to him...that's all I'll ever be in his eyes..."

"Now, don't dismiss that friendship so quickly, dear. Right now he *needs* exactly that: a friend. But if you do feel more, be honest when the opportunity *does* present itself. Helaine, please look at me..." When she finally met my gaze, I could see pools of unshed tears in her eyes. I remembered all too well how painful it was to keep those tears bottled up, letting them overstay their welcome in my attempt to be brave and strong. "Camille not only broke his heart...Because of her, Antoin's lost hope of ever being appreciated for who he is. Not just an artist, but as a human being. If you really want your gift to stand out, don't have it speak to his art. Let it speak to his *heart*, from *your* heart..." I paused, offering a gentle smile and a dab at her first tears with my thumb. "If you really want to do the fudge, make it so when he takes a bite, he'll know everything will be alright. And if you do the scarf, choose colors and a pattern that reflects what he means to you. Make it so when he wraps up in it, he'll know he's safe with the warmth of your friendship. Then, even if he never returns your feelings, he'll still remember you and that you cared for him in this dark, lonely period of his life."

"Will...you help me with both...?"

"I'll help a little, dear, but it must come only from you and your own heart." I smiled more, thinking to myself that I also didn't want Erik to accuse me of meddling.

****

Christmas Eve night found Erik and I wide awake, our excitement over the coming day heightened to a new level than we'd ever felt, save perhaps for our first Christmas as true husband and wife. Our anticipation was silent, however, until I realized the dance in his eyes was not just an imagined reflection of my own thoughts. "What on earth are you smirking at?" I giggled.

"Am I? I was going to point out your own smirk, my dear...it's contagious..."

"Oh, is that it?" I pushed myself up into a sitting position. "I know this season always puts you in a cheerful mood, love, but tonight you're absolutely giddy!" I planted myself sideways on his lap then, resting my hands on his shoulders. "You know something, and it's not just what you yourself placed under the tree!"

"Are you saying that's *your* cause for smirking?" He challenged, raising an eyebrow.

"Oh, no! You're not getting it out of me that easily!" I retorted, then unsuccessfully stifled a gasp when I realized I'd pushed *that* button of his. And there was no turning back.

"Ah, so you *are* hiding something from the O.G.!" Eyes flashing with his old mischievous side, he wrapped his arms around me tightly, my neck now mere inches from his growling lips.

"So *you* admit that I *can* hide things from you? My, you've lost your touch..." The taunting words spilled out before I could stop them, and as a result, they were followed immediately by a squeaky giggle. "I suppose I deserved that..." I turned my head so I could stop his lips with mine. "But try as you might, I gave my word I would say nothing. As for *your* secret..."

"Oh, no! Fair's fair!" He chuckled, brushing his lips against mine. "Besides, I refuse to get your hopes up."

"I *knew* it!" I clapped.

"Well then we both have just given away the general direction of our secrets, haven't we?" He moved his fingers through my hair as his smirk grew all the more.

"Apparently..." I slid my hand around his pajama collar to the back of his neck. "Let us leave the details til morning..."

"Mm...fair's fair..." He dropped his hand to caress my side. "Til morning, my dear..."

"Any idea as to how to pass the time?" I teased.

"Oh, my dear, you forget...the idea was all yours..."

"You're right...I *did* say something about making a special batch of brownies to go with tomorrow's dinner..." I giggled and started to get up. I cannot say which sound that followed was louder: his growl or my squeal as he pulled me back into bed.

****

****TEN****

The next morning, we proceeded with our usual tradition of sharing a light breakfast before exchanging gifts with each other. Claire, Henri, and the rest of the Giry family would be joining us later on for dinner and singing carols, and plans were already in the works to attend the DeChagneys' annual New Years party. This morning, however, it was just for us, and we felt so blessed to have Antoin home and Helaine joining us as well.

As Erik pushed his chair back from the table, he dabbed his mouth before lowering the napkin to reveal his smirk starting to return. "Now then, who shall be first with the gifts?" He led the way into the living room.

"Since there are more of us this year, why don't you hand them out? Antoin can take on the role of Pere Noel with the others later." I placed the dishes by the sink before joining them. Thankfully, Antoin and Helaine were too focused on their own nervousness to notice our playful hinting.

"A wonderful idea, my dear!" Erik grinned before handing Helaine a rather large but flat wrapped package; Antoin gave himself away as the giver by looking up, eyes wide. He leaned forward in his seat, watching her open it while at the same time looking as though he were readying a million excuses or apologies. Her reaction, however, told him he had nothing to fear as she held up the painting; he had captured her sewing by the fireplace, a look of sheer peace and contentment on her face.

"It's—when…?" She glanced over in awe at the artist, who then cleared his throat shyly.

"A few weeks after you arrived…I'd started to fetch a bedtime snack when I saw you there…You just looked so…at-home….it pleased me to know that you felt so warm and comfortable here already…so welcomed…"

"I do feel all of that…even more now…" she smiled, carefully setting the canvas down next to her. "Thank you…"

"Merry Christmas…" He returned the smile warmly; Erik allowed a silent moment to pass between them before he spoke up.

"Antoin…" He selected Helaine's parcel next, placing it into our son's arms.

"Do I smell a hint of sweetness?" Antoin grinned over at Helaine, his eager fingers already working on the strings and ribbons.

"You might…" Helaine giggled at his childlike demeanor. It wasn't long before the rips in the brown paper revealed the scarf I'd watched her knit. The craftsmanship of the piece itself or even the pattern alone could be deemed noteworthy; it was the colors she chose, however, that caused it to really stand out. Stripes of dusky pinks, purples, reds, and oranges blended subtly together while the edges were bordered by golden yellow and silvery gray. The inspiration was fairly obvious, and yet the look in Antoin's eyes demanded an explanation.

"Sunrise? Or sunset…?"

"Both…" Helaine smiled more shyly. "I've seen you many times wander out to see both…when I wake up early to start breakfast or am finishing the evening dishes…I know they both mean something to you…I figure sunset for a time of reflection, but sunrise for the hope a new day brings. Both are important…it's good to look back at the lessons of the past, but we must also be ready to embrace the future…"

"You're...a wise woman, Helaine. My parents have taught you much..." Tears filled our son's eyes as he gently grasped Helaine's hand, lightly pecking her knuckles. "Thank you..."

"Don't forget the fudge, silly..!" Helaine tearfully blushed, unwrapping the scarf from around the tin of chocolate.

"Only a gift as thoughtful as this could cause me to neglect perfectly good sweets!" Antoin laughed, already sinking his teeth into the first piece before handing a second morsel to her. "Absolutely delectable..." His compliment caused her face to redden more, and Erik took that as a cue to move on.

"Speaking of hope, I was saving this poem for when the others arrive, but I figure there's no more fitting time than now to share it..." He went over to his desk and retrieved a sheet of paper from the top drawer. Clearing his throat, he read it with every emotion it required:

"One Star

Blanket of darkness
Over endless desert sands
One star shining
One lonely dot of light
Leading...Drawing...Guiding...

One hope
Given out of Love Himself
One tiny Newborn of flesh
Destined for sacrifice

One death
Giving us life
Giving us peace
Giving us that same hope
Shining through us
Leading...Guiding...
Drawing other wanderers
Other travelers
To Love Himself
To the very Source
Of all they seek

All it takes
Is one star of hope
In the blanket of darkness
Over this vast wilderness
One light..."

"Oh, Erik...just when I think there's no possible higher level of admiration I could have for your work..." I beamed, pulling him into a kiss.

"Papa?" Antoin stood then. "I now know what direction my art must take. This faith you and Mama have raised me up in...I don't know why I didn't see it before...how it's more of a part of me than even my art. I want to *make* it my art...paint His Creation in a way that would point to its Maker..."

"He *gave* you that gift, my son...I have no doubt He will help you do just that..." Erik gave his shoulder a firm squeeze. "But now, speaking of gifts, shall we open more before you retreat to your canvas?"

"Of course!" Antoin chuckled, returning to his seat.

****

In the days leading up to New Years' Eve, Antoin fully embraced his newfound determination for his artwork, producing the first of an announced series only the next afternoon. It was a simple landscape, almost entirely black-and-white. The sky held the only colors of a sunrise or sunset, with the smudged and faded outline of a hand holding a paintbrush over the hued stripes and clouds. He explained that the inspired series, entitled 'Fingerprints', would showcase the Hand of God in various seasons and circumstances; his enthusiasm over the whole prospect was contagious, and we expressed our eagerness to see what God put in him to paint next.

His interactions with Helaine, however, were almost the complete opposite of his excitement; he was much more subdued around her, his words abrupt and few. To be sure, he treated her kindly. It was clear to Erik and I especially that he was simply nervous, and after the third day of this, he vowed to take Antoin out for a shopping errand in town so that he could make sure our son wasn't once again following his footsteps down a road paved with missed opportunities and fear. "Besides," he smiled at me after laying out his plan, "you ladies deserve the perfect accessories for your New Years' gowns..."

"Just don't go overboard this time...We don't want to take attention away from the Vicomtesse..."

"A little late for that, my dear. You've already stolen all of mine..." He lightly caressed my face.

"Oh, you know what I mean!" I playfully flinched away. "Go easy on him though. His nervousness is understandable..."

"Of course. But she has yet to give him reason to stay there. Nor did you give *me* reason. The blinders of past pain must come off..."

"I know they do." I stepped into his arms, kissing him before resting my head against his chest with a sigh. "I just hope they come off easily..."

"I'll do everything I can to ensure that, my dear..." He gently rubbed my back. "I stood in his place once. I know what I needed to hear then, and so I know what he needs now." Before the subject could be discussed further, Helaine quietly knocked on our door to announce breakfast was ready.

****

As per tradition, the DeChagneys succeeded in outdoing themselves from the prior New Years' Eve balls with the current one. It was a night special to the both of them, being so near to the anniversary of their engagement; though that first year's ball together had ended in fear, they chose to embrace it as a chapter in their love. Christine had previously explained that the first ball was what they considered the first true test of how far they were willing to go for each other. For herself, it had been the opportunity she needed to be confident and comfortable enough to kiss him openly, to show the other guests where they stood. For Raoul, it was a moment of protection...a chance to show that his promise of her safety wasn't merely words, but actions.

Of course, it had taken Erik a few years to fully accept being not just included, but welcomed just as much as everyone else, and it was the DeChagney daughters who had finally convinced him. I remember so clearly how they would each take a hand, pulling him into their playful and carefree dances. Once their bedtime came, however, it had been my turn to wrap my arms around him, to be the only witness to his breathless release of emotion upon my shoulder as he pulled me all the closer, if only to steady himself.

"Do you know something?" Madame Giry set down her glass, bringing me back to the present. She and I were taking a break while Erik danced with Claire.

"What is it?" I took my eyes off of the father and daughter pair to focus on the older woman and to keep my sleepy mind from drifting away again.

"I taught your husband how to dance."

"Really?" My astonishment was genuine, although I really should have guessed.

"We were young...It was perhaps a few years after I brought him to the opera house. I was showing him a new routine, as I frequently did, and out of the blue he asked me to teach him. I suppose he was perhaps jealous that I possessed a talent that he had yet to learn or even try, and so I obliged him. Oh, he was clumsy at first...unsure and awkward. He nearly gave up and sent me away. Then I told him he already knew half the secret, with how he naturally absorbed music like a sponge to water. The rest was to let the music inside move through him...flow through his limbs as freely as it flowed through his soul. He learned quickly after that, but then he tucked it away for lack of use." She lowered her gaze then to take a sip. "The next time I saw a glimpse of that skill was the night of Don Juan Triumphant. That's when I truly knew it was him on that stage."

It must have really been tucked away... I thought to myself, recalling how he'd once named dancing as the one talent he lacked. She seemed to be wrestling within herself over saying more to me, but was forced to put the idea aside as Antoin approached us. "Might I steal my mother away for a dance?"

"Oh, of course!" Antoinette motioned us both to the dance floor, and as we fell in step with the number being played, Antoin cleared his throat.

"I've...decided to ask Helaine for her hand in marriage, provided you approve, of course, as her employer and guardian..."

"Oh, my son, that's wonderful!" I hugged him, pecking his cheek as a signal of my blessing.

"I've not decided when though. I thought of midnight tonight, but at the same time I don't wish to overshadow the DeChagneys' reason for celebration..."

"I'm sure Christine would be thrilled to have another couple sharing in their happiness for the New Year. If you'd like to be sure, I could ask..."

"Please?" He looked at me with the same anxious eyes I'd seen so many times on Erik's face. It was a look that always went straight to my heart, causing me to move whatever mountains I could to ease their concern.

"Of course I will..." I gave his shoulder a reassuring squeeze.

When the opportunity arose shortly afterwards to voice Antoin's request and concern to our hosts, the couple needed no time to discuss it before they agreed. "As a matter of fact, the speech I've prepared for this year will give him the perfect lead-up for it." Raoul grinned. "It's actually close enough to midnight...Perhaps I'll give it now..."

"Marvelous! Thank you both!"

"Oh, believe me, the pleasure's all ours...to see the same love flowing into the next generation is the sort of success that surpasses all the riches of this world..." Christine beamed. At that, Raoul moved to the stairs and cleared his throat, and I quickly made my way to Erik's side.

"Ladies and gentlemen, it's that time again when I formally wish you all the best as we enter the New Year. Most of you already know why this occasion means so much to the Vicomtesse and I, but what we don't speak of nearly enough is how much we hope that you all can share in our celebration by making it your own. You see, the love we share with those around us shouldn't be held back from being expressed save for the special days. Love, when it's true, *makes* each day special. So as the clock ticks down and brings us into the year nineteen-oh-six, I want us to take hands with someone....it could be a spouse, a parent or child...brother, sister, cousin, friend...if they mean something to you at all, then tell them. With new years...with every new day...there comes so much uncertainty. The future is better faced when we have someone right by our sides to face it with us. So friends, let today be the start of making each and every day a special one simply because that love is felt and shared and made known. Let us walk into the new year with arms wide open to embrace each other and the blessings each one brings to our lives. Thank you!" The applause that followed was soon interrupted by Antoin making his way through the crowd to the stairs, Helaine in tow. Choosing to not acknowledge their audience, let alone explain to them, he kept his eyes on her. I tightened my grip around Erik's arm in excited anticipation, causing him to let out a low chuckle only I could hear.

"Helaine, I...hadn't planned to do this publicly...I didn't write any speeches or even think much about the words I'd choose to say....That's a gift of my mother's that I did not inherit. More like my father, I let my art speak for me. But...what the Vicomte said...the uncertainty of my future...it brought to mind something my father told me. There were times he felt like a pile of shattered glass...broken and useless...That's exactly how I felt for most of this past year. All the plans I thought were coming together so perfectly were flung to the ground. Everything I thought was for certain turned out to be a lie.

"But then, Papa further explained that while we're all broken at one or more points in our lives, we don't have to stay that way. With God as the Master Artist, we can let others come into our lives and help pick up those pieces...form them into the beautiful mosaic we were meant to be. Mama did that for him. I watched their love constantly as I grew up. At first it was with admiration...Then, when my heart got broken, it was with envy and bitterness. But then you came along, Helaine. You, with your light and your hope...it wasn't invasive...it was gentle and natural...you offered your kindness and friendship with not one hint towards requesting or expecting anything in return. You were there...*just* there, but you were *there*...and I don't want to take for granted that you'll always be there; helping my parents is only going to be one chapter in your life..."

"Did our son just imply we're nearing death's door with our age?" Erik jokingly muttered.

"Hush..." I suppressed a giggle through my joyful tears, gently nudging his side with my elbow.

"For the other chapters and even part of this one, Helaine, I hope that I may share in whatever God has in store. I would be greatly honored if you would be my wife. Will you marry me?" As he knelt down, the clock began to chime in the new year.

"For...a man who claims to be ungifted with words..." Helaine wiped at her tears. "Of course I'll marry you, Antoin!" Flinging her arms around him, she helped him up so that they could share a proper embrace and first of many more midnight kisses. The vision of them was soon blocked as Erik stepped in front of me to follow our son's lead.

****

####***ELEVEN***####

The wedding was set for late the following spring, allowing for ample time to make preparations. Once Janelle received the news, she responded immediately with plans to return to France a month early so that she could help wherever she was needed. What we didn't expect when we met their ship was to find her, Samuel, and the children being accompanied by none other than Carlotta and Betzazel! Adding to our astonishment, Carlotta was out of her wheelchair, using a cane and barely showing awareness of anyone who might be staring. Her eyes and bright smile were kept mostly locked on her former stagemate, and it wasn't long before I caught a glimpse at her reason. "How good to see you looking so well!" I greeted her with a warm embrace, then lowered my voice to a whisper. "Is that a new ring I see?"

"It is!" The former diva beamed, showing the diamond off excitedly. "His toy-making business really took off over Christmas. This was the first thing he wanted to buy. I still cannot believe I'm able to feel this way again!"

"Congratulations to you both on a well-deserved life of happiness!" I grinned. "Do you have a date in mind?"

"No...on that we cannot agree..." She sighed, though her smile lingered. "The sooner the better in my opinion, but he insists on giving me the celebration he says I deserve...the one I was never able to have with–" she shook her head, but her watering eyes betrayed her.

"I might have an idea, if you trust me..."

"How can I not trust you with how well my daughter turned out?" She grasped my hands reassuringly.

"I'll have to run it by a few others first. If they approve, I'll fill you in."

****

When the day finally came, there were two grooms watching in anticipation for their brides to make their appearances, with Erik escorting Helaine, and Samuel leading Carlotta. The younger couple was thrilled to let the elder pair hijack their plans, and much to Erik's and my total shock, Carlotta barely had an opinion to voice about the decorations. Her feelings toward Betzazel truly did run far deeper than pity or guilt, I realized. All the questions I might have had about how their relationship unfolded failed to matter the moment I laid eyes on their true happiness, reflected in the way they silently communicated. I was so proud of Erik, and during the reception, I made it a point to tell him so...proud of him for suppressing his old instincts enough to listen and understand Carlotta, and for allowing those same old instincts to rise up again just enough to show Betzazel his full potential and value. "That wasn't me entirely..." he tried to shrug it off as he dipped me halfway through the dance number.

"No, but...if there were another love language you'd be gifted with, it would be the language of observance and discernment. You may not have known, let alone asked for it, but you choose to use it with a wisdom that comes from the same Source. You choose to set aside your own wishes and opinions and pour out exactly what is needed. God does the heavy lifting, it's true. But don't disregard the baby steps you take as well..." With that, the music ended, and we applauded the band before returning to our seats.

"Well, don't *you* disregard the impact *you've* made, my dear...Not just on me, but on everyone here." He motioned generally to the crowd under the canopy. "You helped Antoinette ease the pain of not having Meg around. You opened the door of friendship between myself and the DeChagneys. You spoke wisdom and guidance into my uncertainty and stubbornness... played a vital role in raising our children... and it was you who motivated me to soften my heart toward Carlotta... made me aware of my needs and worth in my own past so that I could bring such awareness to Betzazel... I know it was the Spirit leading you, Sarah, but you acted upon it. And now, look around you...look at us...look what we have accomplished just by being willing to surrender to His Will..."

"Oh, Erik!" I wrapped my arms around him then, leaving tender kisses all over his face. "Just you wait, my love...Despite how old our children make us feel, our story is far from over..."

****

Indeed, our story certainly was far from over. Antoin and Helaine decided to stay close by rather than move to Paris, citing the wealth of inspiration Antoin received from our surroundings. He built them a small cottage a few yards away from the main house with Erik's help. As an additional wedding gift, we cleared our things out of the work shed so that Antoin could turn it into his studio.

To our great delight, Carlotta and Betzazel chose to live out their marriage in Paris, making new, better memories of the city. As a result, Janelle and Samuel relocated their family to Paris as well and were immediately welcomed into the Opera House, where Samuel became one of the new stagehands. While Joseph and Lydia followed Janelle's interest to the stage, Ethan stepped in to tutor all the young performers in academics and literature.

As with most times of joy and celebration, however, times of sorrow sooner or later follow, challenging us to hold onto that joy a little longer and a little tighter. Nine years after the double wedding, we received word that the DeChagneys would no longer be able to host anymore New Years parties, due to Raoul's declining health. Clutching my chest at the news, I looked at Erik through stinging tears. We knew. I had seen the beginnings of Raoul's symptoms early on, recognizing them as a disease my father would suffer from, but I was unable to say anything for fear of revealing anything before they were supposed to be discovered. And although the black-and-white scenes from the movie had prepared us for what was to come, we were still devastated two years later when Christine succumbed to a sudden illness. Weakened by her sacrificial care and concern for her husband's condition, she was unable to fight it.

Just as he was forced to vow, Erik placed the rose and, with my full blessing, the ring on her grave with trembling hands. He did not speak for several days after, nor did I coax him. I simply knew that despite the deep, unshakeable love between us, Christine still meant so much to him as a dear friend. She had been his comfort and the first hint of light and hope that he needed long before I entered the picture. And so I held him through the nights that followed, offering my shoulder to cry on or my silent companionship when his tears were spent but sleep refused to come.

He eventually recovered, but things were never the same after. He moved around a little bit slower, always looking older and more tired. To be sure, there were many countless moments that brought a smile to his face, watching our family grow with new grandchildren and attending performances at the Opera House.

One of the more bittersweet occasions was seeing Claire's son, Philippe, marry Gustaave DeChagney's daughter Alyce. Erik was thrilled, as was Meg, that now all three family trees were linked together. They wept together discussing how Christine would have felt about it, and how they hoped she was smiling down upon the union.

Raoul did not live long enough to hold any great-grandchildren. His heartbreak over Christine's death only served to increase his symptoms. We took comfort in knowing his passing was peaceful, surrounded by family. This time, however, I was the one to ponder longer over his death, my mind weaving connections between Raoul, my father, and what I was now starting to see in Erik. Although I doubted he had the exact same condition, there were other signs of something that would only worsen over time. As a coping method and to keep myself from burdening him with the weight of my thoughts, I jotted them down in a poem, making copies for each of our children so that when the time was right, they could see and learn from my response:

The Mask of Age

The hands that once braided my hair
And caressed my face so tenderly
Now tremble
Clenched into fists of frustration
As they can no longer grip a brush or pen

The eyes that focused so attentively
On music notes and works of art
He crafted
Now struggle to see past blurred lines and shadows
Without the aid of the light he once despised.

The arms that once held our children
With such gentle strength
The legs that once ran after them
As playful laughter filled the air
Can now no longer lift
Or carry him above a shuffled step

Childhood nightmares blend with memories
In the mind that soaked in every subject
And book that he read
Wrinkles outnumber scars
Lungs that carried beautiful songs
Now labor with every breath

Time has stolen much

But my love for this man
Has done all except to weaken with age

For the man I fell in love with
Still exists deep inside
Past the wrinkles
And weakened muscles
The softened voice
Still whispers, "I love you"
When the nightmares no longer cloud his mind
The faded eyes
Still shine and serve
As a window into his loving heart
Those fingers which can no longer grip
Still brush away my tears
When in a moment the day's trials
Become so hard to bear
And in that same moment
I remember
Age is merely yet another mask
A disguise that he's unable to shed

Time has stolen much
But our love for each other
Has done everything except weaken
With age.

****

"Claire? Henri, what a surprise!" I opened the door wider to let them in out of the warm summer downpour. It was now 1928, and although age had not overtaken me as much as it had affected Erik, I still struggled with getting around, the injuries I'd sustained in the shipwreck had returned in the form of arthritis. "You just missed Helaine and Antoin, else they would have answered the door..."

"We'll be sure to visit them next and see how Juliette is coming along with her wedding plans..." Claire grinned before hugging me, and I paid the drenched state of her clothes no mind. "I know it's not the most ideal day for traveling, Mama, but...I felt it couldn't wait..." She lowered her gaze, her smile fading.

"It's...Henri's grandmama, isn't it...?" My daughter merely nodded, and Henri cleared his throat, placing a steadying hand on her shoulder despite the redness around his own eyes.

"Mama and Papa are with her now, but I'm afraid we can't stay here long. I know it would be a lot for the two of you to make the journey..."

"It would..." I sighed, my eyes already watering.

"How is Papa?" Claire hesitantly asked.

"He has more bad days than good, unfortunately..." I admitted. "It's the nights that he struggles with most of all...Nightmares he thought he left behind decades ago..." At that, Claire reached over and gently took my hand.

"I'm sorry we don't visit more often..."

"Nevermind, child...you're here now..." I offered a brave smile. "Would you like to see him?"

"I'd love to, Mama, of course!" She opened her purse, retrieving an envelope. "Grandmama wanted me to give you this. I suggest reading it away from Papa...Even if he could understand its contents or what's going on with her, it would only break him more..."

"That's so thoughtful of you, Claire..." I took the letter, giving her another hug before leading them to one of the spare bedrooms which now housed the library as well as Erik's instruments. He was sitting at the piano now, arms at his side as he gazed out the window; his eyes were on the pouring rain, yet they were distant, as if his mind were worlds away. "My love..." I approached him cautiously, not knowing if what was going through his thoughts would cause him to startle at my sudden presence. "Claire and Henri are here..." I touched his hand, and he turned his head to face me.

"Claire..." he whispered, and just the mention of her name brought new life to his face. Although he and Janelle held a special bond, Claire would always be his baby girl, having developed more of a caregiving nature than the other two. She always seemed to know just what we needed and the exact moment to give it, and as they greeted each other, I knew she was giving me a chance to read Antoinette's letter while keeping her father in the present. Reluctant to leave the sight of them, I ducked out of the room and closed myself into our bedroom. Lowering myself to a chair, I took a deep breath before opening the piece of paper.

"*My dear friend Sarah,*

What I am about to write has been on the tip of my tongue for years, but the opportunity remained out of my reach. Now, however, I feel as though it cannot wait any longer. I believe you will wish to keep it the secret that it has been, even from your own children, and so my only explanation to Claire will be that it is a final message between friends.

There is no easy way to say this, and so I will be direct. I know about your true origins. At first, my doubts about your story and how you and Erik met were based solely on little things, such as Christine's description of how you were dressed when you first met her, and how you lacked basic skills and knowledge in helping me keep house. I thought surely you would know those things even being from America in this particular period of time. Then, when I saw the pendant around your neck, my suspicion was confirmed.

You see, before I laid eyes on Erik at that gypsy fair, I had seen those trinkets being sold. I heard all about how they were supposed to be magical and transport the holder anywhere they wanted to go. It seemed to be too good to be true, and so I passed it by. When I caught a glimpse of one in Erik's hand as we were making our escape, I decided not to voice my doubts. I knew he needed every bit of hope he could get.

I of course don't know the true details of where or even when you are from, Sarah. Nor do I expect to learn them now. I know that with how happy you have made Erik, it really does not matter how it happened. I just want you to know how much I have admired watching the both of you learn to love each other and raise your children into the man and women they have become.

It has been a great joy and an honor to have you as my friend. I am fully aware that this very well may be my last goodbye to you, but I also know that it is only a temporary one, as we share the faith and hope in what is to come.

Pass my love on to your husband for me. He might not be able to process losing me, but one can never hear that they are loved too often.

Take care of you both.

Your friend,
Antoinette"

    It took me several moments to let my tears run their course. They were stilled prematurely, however, when I heard soft music playing from down the hallway. Wiping at the salty streaks trickling down my face, I crept toward the beautiful sound, peering into the library to see Erik completely back in his element, eyes closed as he swayed to music that was too deep within himself to forget entirely. Claire had her hand on his shoulder for support as she quietly sang along; though she never took to the stage, she had still developed a decent amount of talent that she preferred to share only with family and close friends.

    I could have burst into tears all over again at the scene before me, this time from joy and pride. Instead, I quietly but hastily fetched my camera, knowing that such moments would be fewer and far between the more Erik's dementia progressed.

    Thankfully, none of them noticed me capturing the candid picture; even Henri, though silent, was holding Claire's other hand from over her shoulder, his free arm wrapped around her waist. When the photographer in me was satisfied, I set aside the camera and slid into the chair closest to the doorway. I did not applaud when the song finished; instead, I approached the three of them, mouthing a 'thank you' to Claire before sitting down on the bench beside Erik, snuggling against him. "That was beautiful, both of you, as always..."

    "It will only be that beautiful with her singing it...I wrote it for her voice..." Erik's voice was distant again, and I chose not to dwell on the question of whether he was speaking of Claire or Christine.

"I agree, my love..." I tenderly kissed his jaw. "Will you play just one more? And then I'm afraid they have to leave for today..."

"A good musician always has an encore prepared..." His face flashed with a trace of his old self, the slightest smile making an appearance before he slid his fingers over the keys, getting a feel for the song he wished to play next. I recognized the tune immediately, and this time, my voice joined Claire's as we filled the room with Psalm thirteen.

****

~~~~~One year later....

I felt your kiss in my dreams that night
In the morning, when I woke, you were gone
My head on your shoulder
Our fingers intertwined between us
But only mine felt my tears as they fell

I can only conclude
That you woke up just long enough to know
And so you used your last breath
Your final ounce of strength
To take care of me
See to my comfort
Make sure I know
Just how much you loved me
If only I could tell you again

But I take comfort in knowing
That our happy ending
Was merely the beginning
Of your eternity
In the Heaven you longed for
So long ago
I take comfort in knowing
Til death do us part
Won't be forever
This goodbye is not farewell
I take comfort in knowing
Our voices will sing together again

This time joined with the choir
Of saints and angels around the Throne
I take comfort in knowing
The peaceful look on your face
Can only be a glimpse
As to how you look now
Your scars, your pain
Your fears, your tears
They are no more

So worry not for me, my love
Though my tears fall now
Our children are here
We'll help each other
Remember you not with sorrow
Instead we'll remember your laugh
Remember your music
Remember your spirit
Remember your love
All that you gave
The memories we made

I take comfort in this
The peace you feel now
Will carry us through

Our happy ending
Is only the beginning
My love

****

My Papa—The Fixer of Broken Things
By Claire Amelia (Dupree) Dubois, 1931

    In going through my parents' things, I've come across what you have just finished reading—their story as painstakingly written down and tucked away by my mother. She never told us children about the existence of such a record...not even on her deathbed six months ago. I don't claim to understand why she would even bother to write such details down that seem so unbelievable in comparison to what we were told and which cannot be proven one way or the other. I can only guess that she wrote it for herself; she was always keeping daily journals on top of writing her occasional poems and short stories, none of which she sought to get published. Perhaps in the back of her mind, she had a hunch this story would be discovered by one of us. Perhaps she wrote it with a subconscious hope that we'd finally know the truth and what to do with it. Now that they are both gone from this world, perhaps it is safe to share, but only with those we can trust.

    So I have decided to make my own contribution to my parents' story. I will then store it all away for perhaps the next generation to find and add to. It's an inheritance with no value except that which is priceless. The truth is both such a great gift and a great burden to carry...knowing that it is a powerful weapon that can hurt both the holder and those around them at any given moment. Sooner or later, however, truth must come out of hiding. It must be told.

    I expect that was my mother's ultimate reason for recording their story. It is also my greatest reason for adding to it, so that you may see a bigger picture, another layer to who my papa really was. I shared it with my mother and my siblings after his passing, and I feel she would approve of me sharing it with you now.

    My papa was always fixing things. I've been told that his home below the opera house was furnished and decorated mostly with that which had been broken or otherwise discarded by the occupants above him. Every single instrument he owned was secondhand, lovingly restored for his music. The boat and the bed had both served their purpose on the stage, and he had rescued them from being destroyed, turning them into works of art with his paint and his carving tools. All his clothes and costumes were once scraps of cloth before he mended them and gave them new purpose and life. Later on, I don't recall more than a few instances where he replaced anything with a brand-new version unless it was absolutely necessary, and even then he took the old and the worn out and turned them into rags for cleaning or wood for heat. Sometimes he would even incorporate them into his artwork so seamlessly one would never mistake a single part as junk or scrap. Never once did he deem a single thing as useless. There was one time when the arm of my favorite doll got snagged on some thorns as I was picking berries, and I pulled so hard to free it, it got torn off completely. I at first brought it to my mother, but she was busy cooking supper. Papa called me over then, and he took the doll so carefully as if it were real. I suppose he saw that she was real to me, at the time. He sewed that arm back on my doll with such tenderness and expertise while I sat at his feet looking on. Not only did he not deem that doll useless, he saw it as loved, because I loved her. He even gave her a kiss on the head before gently handing her back to me, never once laughing at my imagination.

    My papa was always fixing more than things. Whenever we fell as we were growing up, he was always first to come running to our aid, scooping us up and bandaging our scrapes and cuts or soothing our bruises. What really healed us though was the way he'd distract us from the pain by singing a song as he danced with us in his arms or feeding us one of mama's sweets. He'd then hold us in his lap, rocking us gently as he told us a story about one of our many animals going on a supposed adventure with humorous but relatable outcomes we could learn from and apply to our own lives.

    When I was a little bit older…old enough for my heart to be broken or to care what other people thought and said of me…he showed me that same tenderness and care as he tried his very best to fix what others had broken. He'd wrap his arms around me, kissing my forehead before humming softly until my tears turned into exhausted sniffles. I remember once, when I was twelve, resting my head on his shoulder as he stroked my hair. A boy I liked at the opera house had moved away, and one of my friends decided to start a rumor about his departure. I had defended him, and she in turn made me a part of that rumor. "I cannot fix this one for you, my little Claire. Not this time. I cannot force them to see and treat you as you truly deserve to be cherished. If I really had that power, my life from childhood would have been very different, and your mother and I would never have met. No, some things are meant to be broken. I had to learn that just as you must learn it."

"But why?" I asked, my eyes welling up again. "Why must it hurt so much if it's meant to be this way?"

"Because, my dear child, we cannot see the reason yet. We only know what we are losing. We don't see what we're about to receive, and so we try to cling when we should really let go."

"Oh, but Papa, Anette is my best friend! At least, she used to be…If Pierre hadn't left, she'd still be a good friend…! Why should I have to let go of that?"

"If she were really as good a friend as you claim, Claire, she would not be treating you this way. If he had indeed stayed, her true colors would eventually come out. Perhaps she, too, liked Pierre…perhaps she is using this rumor to mask her bitterness and heartbreak that he's gone. If he had stayed, she would have turned your friendship into a competition to win his affection."

"She *did* seem to change the subject when I talked about him…" I recalled aloud. "It still hurts, Papa…knowing she's not the friend I thought she was…"

"I know, Claire. I, too, had a friend that turned out to be my enemy. And I had to be broken in order to see the truth, so that I could embrace true friendships that were waiting for me."

"Did it hurt long?"

"Only as long as I kept clinging, dear child. When we do let go, we fall into the arms of the One who *can* fix what's broken and make things right."

"How can things be right if they're meant to be broken?"

"Mosaics and stained glass, dear child. It doesn't take much studying to see that they are made up of broken pieces, but are admired as whole works of art. The masterpiece that is your life is far from completion,

Claire. There will be more breaking. More pain. And though it hurts me and it hurts God to see you hurting, we also believe in you reaching your full potential. He more than anyone knows where He will be taking you on this journey. He is the Author and the Master Artist of your life. When you let go of what you're clinging to, He won't let you fall far. You must trust Him to do the fixing in this case, because I am unable to do it myself." He prayed with and for me then, talking to God in the same candid, open way that we conversed with *him*. We soon turned the focus of the prayer off of my pain and onto Pierre and Anette, that God would fix what might be broken in their lives right then or in their futures.

    I remember feeling so much peace after that talk. The next day, however, took his wise words even further. Mama and Papa took Antoin and I shopping. We were walking by one store that sold art and antiques from all over the world. In the window was a display of pottery from Japan. We would not have noticed any of it, however, were it not for the jagged lines of gold throughout each piece. They'd obviously been broken, but instead of being discarded or restored in a way that would hide the cracks, the artists had made a point to showcase the flaws in such costly beauty. I remember the look in my father's eyes that day. I remember how my mother so lovingly brushed her fingers against the lines on his face, seeming to know exactly what he was thinking. We went inside, and the shopkeeper explained that it was a form of art called Kintsugi, where the gold used to repair and showcase the pottery also serves to strengthen it more. Once my father recovered from his shock at this information, he looked at me, tears still shining on his face. "You see, my dear child?" I remember him whispering as he knelt down in front of me. "When we put our broken pieces in His Hands, He makes us better…stronger…than we ever could have been before…Our pain means that we are learning…growing…And it's that growth and knowledge that makes us stronger. It's growth and knowledge that are as precious as gold…too valuable to lose…You, my dear little Claire, are so valuable that God wants to showcase all that he has done and is doing in your life. Never forget what He is teaching you through everything you experience."

    I did indeed let go of my friendship with Anette, at least the friendship that I had known up until the rumor started. For a time, we distanced ourselves from each other. Then one day she confided in me that she'd written to Pierre, only to find out he was in love with someone else. She was sorry for the rumor, sorry for hurting me and for losing me. We remained good friends after that, up until this very day. My father was right, though, to convince me to let go. Because I did, I learned the meaning of true friendship and how to be warm and loving while still showing wisdom and discernment. In a sense, I had let go of what I *thought* friendship was supposed to be, so that I could take hold of the truth.

It was one of many, countless lessons my father taught me. I just love that even though God is the ultimate Author of Life, He gave my mama the ability to write His Truth into her words. He is the Master Artist, and yet gave my papa and my brother the eyes and hands to see His Works and transfer them onto canvas and into sculptures for others to take notice, not for their glory, but to give Him the credit He's due.

And although God is the ultimate Fixer of Broken Things, He gave my papa the capability and the inspiration to do the same thing on a much smaller scale. He took my papa's broken pieces and used them to give him compassion and awareness....to see what others don't....the value that others might discard. My papa fixed broken things with his artistic talent, but his repairs won't last for all eternity. The broken things he fixed serve as an illustration...serve to point in the direction of the One Who can truly repair permanently and completely. My papa fixed what was broken in me by showing me the truth and pointing me down the correct path. He would never claim the credit though. He only always pointed upward to the Source of all his talents and gifts and wisdom, to His Heavenly Father and mine.

Our Papa is the Fixer of Broken Hearts and Broken Souls. My papa is at rest now. His work is done. Our Papa, however, has so many more souls and hearts to repair. My hope and prayer is one that I believe my mother also had for whoever did in fact find and read through their story...that you, dear one reading this, seek out the Truth, and let go of your brokenness so that The Fixer, The Author, The Artist, will turn your life into His Masterpiece.

The Family Tree

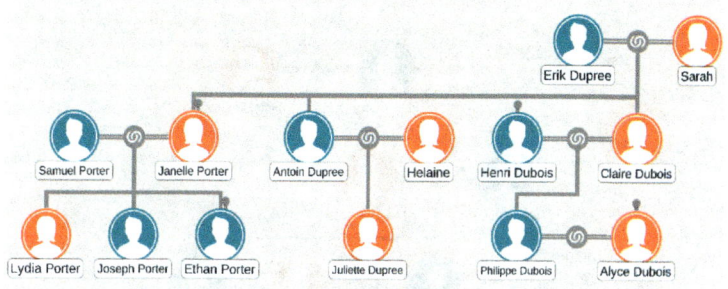

The Adoptions

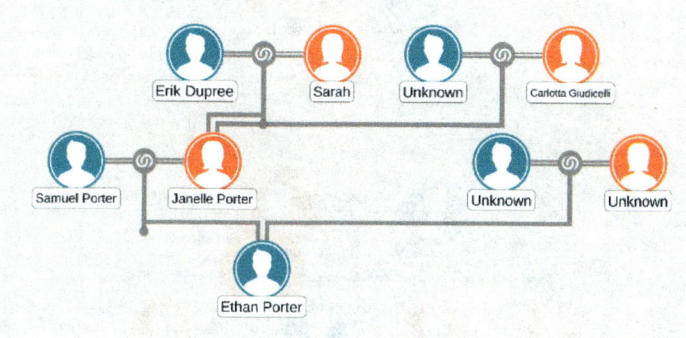

The DeChagney and Giry Connections

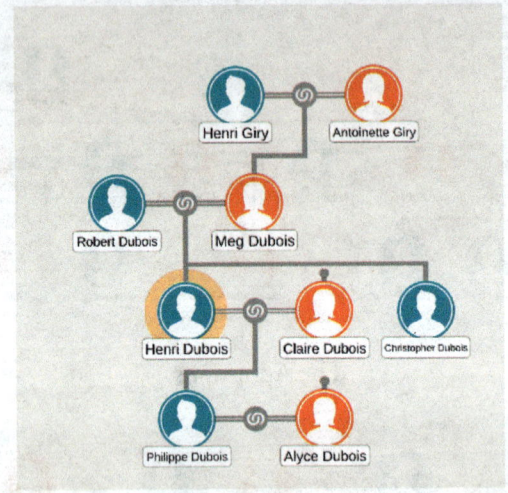
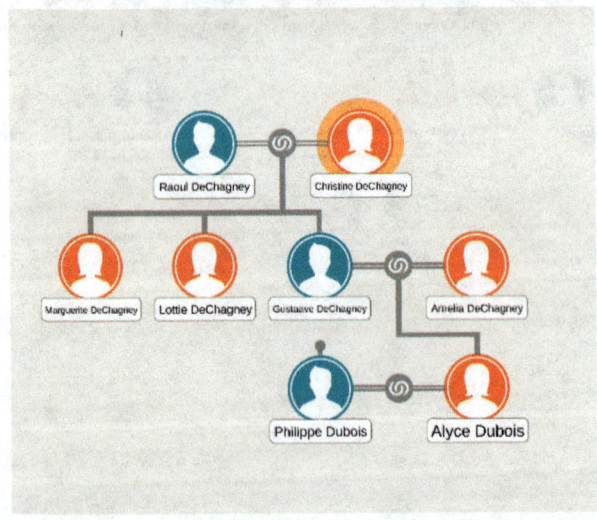

A Final Word

First of all, dear readers, thank you so much for coming along on this journey with me. I have much enjoyed exploring the possibilities of the great "what if", and writing for Erik and I growing old together....fictitiously of course! In truth, I have not experienced married life myself, and so I based our relationship purely on observance. I am surrounded by true-life examples, both near and far, and I also drew inspiration from various tv couples. And so this wasn't just another writing project, but a learning experience for myself.

As I stated at the beginning of this book, this story has been a multi-year project. What started out as merely a comedic idea quickly turned into a dramatic romance, then a sort of multi-generational family saga. You might notice that I chose to mention bits of real history, but omitted at least one major event—WWI. Believe me, I was very, very tempted to incorporate it—to see what impact it might have had on our family at the time. However, as the 2004 film took liberties with setting the majority of events in a year that would not have worked within the context of history, I chose to take liberties of my own. I simply didn't see anything beneficial to my story coming from including a war. I suppose the theory I finally settled on is this:

The moment Erik and I met, our 'worlds'—fiction and real—began to sort of merge and collide. Some of real life history stayed with me, but mostly, I became a fictitious character myself, and so I became a part of his world. This is why the island where we took refuge after the shipwreck probably couldn't be found on any map, and why we all just happened to speak the same language throughout (aside from Carlotta's occasional Italian expression) As for the few month's difference between my world and arriving at the DeChagney estate, it might be because someone from the future unexpectedly traveled with Erik back to his. I don't pretend to know if that works out logically, but it makes sense in my mind! ●

I suppose some might call this laziness on my part, but in truth, I am not much into the whole sci-fi or fantasy genre, either reading or writing. And so I took many, many artistic liberties to just keep my story going. I truly hope that you can just enjoy the simplicity and suspension from reality, just as much as I have in writing it.

DISCLAIMER:

As with most of my stories, I try to incorporate my Christian faith. This story is no exception, yet I feel the need to clarify. While magic plays a fairly important role in how this story plays out, it is NOT what the One True God uses. He is all-powerful and still performs miracles that cannot otherwise be explained except for His doing, however the Bible is clear about how He feels towards magic/mysticism/sorcery, etc. I use it in this story in the same sort of way that C.S. Lewis used it in his Narnia stories. That particular aspect is pure fantasy. What is absolutely true is the message of His promises, love, forgiveness, and grace. I encourage you to read and study the Scriptures for yourselves to discover what may or may not be truth. My prayer is that in giving Erik hope, I convey the same hope and truth and love to each one of you. May you truly find the deepest, purest form of inner peace.

Patches, my beloved, accidentally-trained "Feline Phantom Phan" and inspiration for Carmella

Made in the USA
Monee, IL
17 November 2025

35020725R00134